The
Philadelphia
Quarry

OTHER BOOKS BY HOWARD OWEN

Howard Owen

The Philadelphia Quarry

THE PERMANENT PRESS
Sag Harbor, NY 11963

For information, address:
    The Permanent Press
    4170 Noyac Road
    Sag Harbor, NY 11963
    www.thepermanentpress.com

Library of Congress Cataloging-in-Publication Data

Owen, Howard—
    The Philadelphia Quarry / Howard Owen.
        pages cm.
    ISBN 978-1-57962-335-7
        1. Reporters and reporting—Fiction. 2. Murder—
Investigation—Fiction. 3. Richmond (Va.)—Fiction. I. Title.

PS3565.W552P55 2013
813'.54—dc23   2013009167

Printed in the United States of America

To Karen, as always

CHAPTER ONE

Monday, January 17

The morgue is self-serve, which isn't the best of news, because some of our reporters are mechanically challenged, and there's no one there to teach them for the third time how to thread the microfilm machine. Watching someone like Ray Long try to do it, Jackson noted once, was like watching a monkey try to fuck a football.

The files for August of 1983 weren't between July and September, of course. They were after April, like someone thought the months should be alphabetized.

But I finally found Richard Slade, at the time of his arrest.

He looked even younger than his seventeen years. I didn't remember that, didn't remember much about it at all.

He wouldn't be convicted until May of the following year, but he never saw unfettered daylight again. Until today.

It is instructive to see what that much prison can do to a man.

The Richard Slade who stands today, waiting for some white man to undo what another one did in 1984, has been reborn— probably, I'm thinking, not in a good way.

He wears glasses now. When he walks, you can see that he has picked up a limp at Red Onion or Greensville that makes him seem old and arthritic. In addition to those twenty-seven-plus years he lost, he's probably aged another ten. But it's the beaten-down aspect that really stands out. Richard Slade, 1983 version, was, from my memory and catch-up reading, a big talker, a smart kid who also was a smart-ass. He would have been called uppity if he'd been born a little earlier. It didn't endear him, I'm sure, to Judge Cain, who wore a Confederate flag tiepin when he drank bourbon at the Commonwealth Club.

Richard Slade, 2011 version, seems as nervous as a cat in a room full of rocking chairs, like a man trying his level best to be humble for fear that anything else might cause him to wake up in his cell after a particularly good dream. When the judge pounds his gavel, he jumps a little. I want to tell him to chill. The Court of Appeals has already issued what they call the "writ of actual innocence." He is exonerated. Unless he shoots somebody here in this dingy-ass courtroom, he's walking.

This judge expresses his regret over the state's mistake. He sounds about as sincere as I'd expect, but he does say the magic words:

"You are now free to go."

An older woman in the seats just behind Slade leans forward and rubs his back. She doesn't cry, or shout hosannas, the way much of what appears to be his family does. The uproar causes the judge to bang his gavel and utter some bullshit about clearing the court, as if everyone can't wait to do just that before he changes his mind. The woman just closes her eyes and rests her forehead against her son's spine.

Philomena Slade has aged more than twenty-seven years, too.

As they leave the old building, the celebration kicks into another gear. Slade's mother is holding on to his right arm, and various people who might be cousins are tugging at him, taking turns hugging him. They are not a petite family, and I fear that some of the more amply endowed women might smother him. Other than the limp, Slade is prison-fit, not an ounce of fat on him.

The state was kind enough to allow him to wear the suit Philomena no doubt bought for him. I guess it's the first time he's worn civilian threads in his adult life.

On Slade's left side is his lawyer. Marcus Green is wearing his usual: a $500 suit and a perpetual frown. Looking at him and Richard Slade, you'd think it was Green who had been done wrong by the state the past twenty-seven years.

Standing next to Green is the Jewish lawyer from Boston who picked Slade out of the sizable lottery of potentially innocent prisoners and took up his cause four years ago. It's taken that long to get from there to here, and I wonder why Slade had to count on some skinny, myopic guy from Up North who talks funny to deliver him.

In addition to the family, there's us, the News Media. I cringe to be a part of this club, clawing and scratching for a piece of the newly freed man. All four local TV stations and a couple from Washington have sent their hairpieces and camera goons over. Then there's our photographer, a couple of freelance reporters and one from the *Post*, and half a dozen guys with iPhones and other high-tech wonders. And here I stand with my notepad. I am the only person out here using a pen and paper. A couple of the young Tweeters are looking at me like I'm some exhibit at the Newseum. "Look! He's even wearing a wristwatch!"

A fight almost breaks out between a couple of the Slade cousins and two of the more obnoxious camera guys, who now look as if they'd like to be somewhere else. A deputy moves in our direction, but then Marcus Green stops at the bottom of the courthouse steps, moves in front of the Boston lawyer, and holds up his right hand. The cameramen and cousins part.

"We are here to celebrate the commonwealth's belated effort to bring justice to an innocent man," Green says, and I can see that he's getting into his preacher mode. "We all know that justice delayed is justice denied. We all know that this man, Richard Slade, has endured the unendurable, left to rot by a system that enslaved and marginalized his ancestors, that came this close"— Green holds his right forefinger and thumb half an inch apart— "this close to burying him alive forever.

"Moses was never allowed to enter the Promised Land, only to glimpse it from afar. Richard Slade is able to walk, proud and free, back to the fresh air and sunshine of freedom."

A "Praise Jesus" escapes from the crowd.

Green stops and pauses for effect. Everything Marcus Green does in public is for effect.

"And there's nothing they can do about it except stand and watch. The police can't keep him from shucking his chains. The courts can't do it. The racist system can't do it." He fails to mention that it was "the system" that just freed him.

Green pauses and looks at me. I'm about ten feet away, half-hidden by a fat guy wielding a fifty-pound camera.

"Not even the news media can do it."

I hear a couple of muttered "amens" and "uh-huhs." Green has managed to turn the crowd's attention toward me. I suppose that I'm the one person here who looks like the stereotype of the newspaper guy.

That's it, Marcus, you asshole. Throw me under the bus.

True, the people I work for haven't been Richard Slade's BFF. There was an editorial back in 1984 that more or less advocated bringing back public hangings. A search in more recent archives, the ones I can bring up on my computer, shows a distinct lack of sympathy for a man who, according to Mr. DNA, did not do it.

Green eventually shuts up. The crowd seems not to know exactly what to do next. Then, one of the cousins announces that they're all invited over to Momma Phil's, "where the real celebration gonna be."

He pauses and looks at all the hunter-gatherers of news and gives his best Mr. T scowl.

"No damn media," he says.

No one's been able to really talk with Richard Slade himself, other than to get a very small sound bite as he left the courthouse.

"Richard! Richard! How does it feel to be free?" some genius journalist shouted as he was being escorted toward the door.

He just looked at the woman who asked the day's dumbest question so far.

"Feels good," was all he said.

Now, as everyone heads toward their cars, Slade and his mother are led by Green to the lawyer's shiny black Yukon.

I've known Marcus Green since the first time he had Richard Slade for a client. I know and he knows that he owes me one after the stunt he's just pulled. Owing and paying are two different things, but it's worth a try.

I slip past one of the cousins and fall into step beside Green, who can only go as fast as Philomena Slade, whose arm he has.

"Can I catch a ride?"

Green acts as if he doesn't know me, then seems amused.

"Willie," he says. "Willie Black. Well, well. I'm surprised that rag you work for is covering this, it being a 'black day for justice' and all."

"I don't write the editorials, Marcus."

It had not been one of our editorial department's finest hours, but, Jesus Christ, it was four years ago.

Back in 2007, when Stephen Fein of Boston first got publicly involved in Slade's case through the Innocence Project and called his first press conference—accompanied by co-counsel Marcus Green—our self-appointed judges were not amused.

The editorial that Green remembers fulminated about the possibility of releasing the man who had committed such a heinous crime.

"It will be a black day for justice," our editorial concluded, "if this scourge is allowed to walk free."

Our newsroom tends to be a bit more liberal than our editorial department ("Fuck," Sally Velez once said when someone presented her with that bit of insight. "What isn't?"), and many wondered if our deep thinkers on the first floor had gone completely tone-deaf.

Now that Richard Slade has been exonerated, those words might as well be etched in stone in the black community. The weekly that has anointed itself as the voice of Richmond's African-American majority actually came up with a good headline last week, when it became clear that this was going to be Slade's own personal Juneteenth: Day for Black Justice.

Green looks at me for a few seconds. Other reporters are trying unsuccessfully to get past what has now become a human cordon around the car.

"C'mon," he says. He gets in the front seat, with the driver. I scurry into the second row, with Richard and Philomena Slade.

We're moving before I introduce myself to them.

Richard Slade doesn't say much. He seems to be concerned with looking out the window like he's trying to remember it all. It can't be more than forty degrees outside, but he lowers his window, after Philomena shows him which button to push.

I ask Slade when exactly he knew for sure he was going to be a free man.

He turns his head back toward me and is quiet for a few seconds.

Finally: "I'm still not sure. Not sure yet. Won't be sure until we get home."

His mother turns to me after I've asked Slade a few more questions.

"What paper?"

"Ma'am?"

"What paper are you from?"

I tell her. I think I hear Marcus Green snort in the front seat.

Her face is hard, as if it has been baked on by her often-solitary battle to free her son.

Finally, she says it. "Get out."

I don't say anything. It's suddenly very warm in here, and I wish I had a smoke.

"Get out! Get out of this damn car!"

Green looks back. I think even he is a little surprised by the sudden violence from this small, self-contained woman. He doesn't care that she has begun to hit and kick me, as best she can in such tight quarters, but I don't think he knew this would happen.

"Careful, Momma," Richard says, trying to quell her, and Green looks concerned for his upholstery.

Finally, he tells the driver to pull over.

"You put him in there!" she's shouting as I slide away from her and out the door in a somewhat frayed district of our fair, care-worn city.

"I'm sorry, man," Green says, trying to stifle a giggle. "But you were the one that wanted a ride."

The car tears away. I pull my cellphone out of my pocket. Sarah Goodnight answers on the fourth ring.

"I need you to come get me." I'm walking toward a street sign and give her the name when I can finally read it.

"Did you get an interview?"

I'm fishing for my cigarettes with my free hand while I answer her.

"More like it got me."

CHAPTER TWO

I pitch the Camel and get into Sarah's Hyundai.

"Rough day?" she asks, either smirking or smiling.

"I've had worse."

I tell her about my morning, and about how much I want to kick Marcus Green's ass.

We go to the hole-in-the-wall across the street from the paper for lunch. No sense in rushing into the day. I forgo a beer, ordering iced tea instead, but then Sarah surprises me by ordering a Miller Lite.

"Are you old enough to drink this early in the day?"

She flips me the bird.

"The way things are going around here, they ought to make beer mandatory," she says.

Sarah's too young to get really cynical about this business, and she hasn't been around newspapers long enough to remember the good times and have a fair basis for comparison. One thing I have learned: You never really appreciate the good stuff when it's here. You take things for granted, things like raises and decent health insurance and the knowledge that your job probably will be there tomorrow.

But Sarah's giving it a good try.

"You know what Grubby wants me to do?"

I offer a guess. She gives me a disgusted look and tells me to keep my mind on a higher plane, that Grubby isn't like that.

Probably not, I concede.

"OK. What, then?"

"He wants to loan me out to SOP."

I suggest that my original guess wouldn't have been as disgusting.

SOP is Sense of Place. It's our version of the special section every newspaper does every year. It's full of stories about various aspects of "our community," whatever that is. By a remarkable coincidence, the stories we do often are about some of the same organizations that buy full-page ads in the section. It comes out every August. We do it because it makes money, but I don't think SOP is ever going to be nominated for a Pulitzer.

Grubby is our publisher, James H. Grubbs. We have a managing editor, but sometimes Grubby can't help himself and has to drill down through about four layers of management and take the hands-on approach.

"I'll have to 'coordinate' with advertising," she wails.

There's not much choice, though. She and I both know that. There are ads on the section fronts, little sticky note ads attached to A1, and ad salespeople sit in on our afternoon meetings. Back in the day, like about six or seven years ago, that would have been about as permissible as pork chops in Mecca.

But we've all found out just how low we'll go when the bottom line is below sea level and health insurance is a privilege instead of a given.

I suggest that she might not ought to refer to our publisher as Grubby.

"Why not?" She takes a swig. "You old farts call him that."

I'm stung. I am too courtly, or not stupid enough, to tell her that I wasn't too old for her on one memorable (for me, at least) occasion. Best not to go there. I am trying to be good, and she probably doesn't even have to try. Hell, she might not remember.

"Well," I say, "we usually try not to say it where he can hear it."

Sarah shrugs. She's twenty-four. She has options. Oh, to be in the don't-give-a-shit years again.

"So," she says, "what're you going to write? I mean, you were there for the trial, right? Back in, like, 1983?"

Eighty-four, I tell her.

"Wow," she says, "that was the year my older brother was born."

"Cool," I reply.

"So, bring me up to speed."

I give her the CliffsNotes version, from what I remember and what I've read in the morgue.

I was younger than Sarah is now when it happened, in my first full year at the paper. I'd worked for them some in college, and they probably hired me because I'd already become a dependable designated driver for some of the older editors, who liked it that I didn't roll my eyes, outwardly at least, when they started telling the old, old stories.

Night cops was what they put you on, still is, when you're low man or woman on the politically incorrect totem pole. How I'm back on that beat is a long story nobody cares or has time to hear.

"It happened the week after Labor Day. They made the arrest late on a Wednesday night, and we didn't hear about it until the next morning.

"I had to rely on the only cop I knew very well at the time, guy named Gillespie . . ."

"Gillespie? The fat guy who's always trying to tell me dirty jokes from, like, 1957?"

Sarah has done a few turns on the night cops beat, trying to work off her natural overload of curiosity and energy.

"Well," I say, forced to semi-defend the indefensible, "he wasn't so bad back then.

"Anyhow, I had to depend on Gillespie to tell me what really happened at the Philadelphia Quarry."

"Wait," Sarah says, setting down her beer. "What the hell is the Philadelphia Quarry?"

"If you can rein in your ADD, all will be revealed."

"I haven't taken Ritalin since I was ten," she says.

That morning, I was hung over. I had gotten off work at one, and then we'd gone over to Jack Wade's house and wound down until we could all fail a Breathalyzer test.

When the phone rang, I'd been asleep maybe four hours. Since it had happened at night, this one still fell to me.

"There was a rape over in Windsor Farms last night," the guy playing adult supervision that morning told me. "Find out what happened."

It got my attention. Most of our serious crime happens in less well-tended neighborhoods. About the worst thing that ever happened in Windsor Farms was some guy would earn himself a DUI coming back from the Commonwealth Club.

"It was at some place called the Quarry."

The place had never been that well-known. One of my neighbors at the Prestwould calls it Richmond's most exclusive club. I was never an invited guest until recently, but I had swam there, sans invitation or trunks, in my youth.

I got dressed and headed out. Jeanette was leaving for work as I brushed my teeth. We had been married a little over a year, and she was still relatively tolerant of the fact that there was a serious time lag between when I got off work and when I returned to our little Bon Air apartment.

I didn't have a lot of great sources yet. I went to Gillespie because he was around the station that morning and I had played five-card draw with him.

"It's still under investigation," he told me.

I assured him that nothing he said would be quoted; I just wanted a starting point. "Just some background."

He looked around and then led me outside.

"I gotta go on patrol. Come on and ride with me."

We left the station, and he started talking.

They had gotten a call sometime after eleven. Somebody was swimming in the Philadelphia Quarry. Just some kids raising hell, but one of the neighbors had complained, and complaints from Windsor Farms were heeded.

When they got there, Gillespie said, the kids ran for it. Most of them were able to get through the break in the fence and disappear into the night. One of them, though, the slowest, or maybe just the one who was farthest out in the water, couldn't get out in time.

"He said that they were out driving around, and then somebody said he knew where they could go swimming in some white guy's pond."

It had been a sticky night, September on the calendar but August on your skin.

They took Richard Slade back to the patrol car, but then the guy with Gillespie had said maybe they ought to take a look inside the fence, check for vandalism.

Gillespie even then was hitting the doughnuts pretty good, and when we arrived at the Quarry that morning and I saw the hole in the fence, I had to smile at the thought of him squeezing his fat ass through.

"So we went inside," he told me, "checked around, gave it the once-over. Then we went over to this shack there, where people changed clothes, I guess.

"And that's where we found her."

Alicia Parker Simpson was sixteen. She was lying on a bench inside the men's changing area. Her arms were tied over her head. The rope was attached to a hook on the wall behind her. Her panties, the only item of her clothing in the room, were stuffed in her mouth.

They managed to find a robe someone had left there. When they helped her to her feet, she told them to please not tell her father.

They asked her who did it, and she sat there, crying and shaking her head.

Finally, Gillespie said he asked her if it was a black guy. They brought Richard Slade over and made him stand a few feet away, outside the open door to the changing room. She was silent for a few seconds, and then Gillespie said she nodded her head.

The hospital confirmed what the cops there already knew, and they charged Richard Slade with rape.

Gillespie told me who she was. We never ran her name in the paper.

I covered the trial, the next spring.

Slade, represented by a court-appointed attorney, never admitted to anything. They interrogated him for a few hours and got nothing but denials. Basically, it was her word against his.

The other guys from the neighborhood, Richard's so-called friends, took a powder. They were made to know that if they falsely claimed that Richard Slade was innocent, that they had only gone to the Quarry to sneak in a late-night swim (and maybe thumb their noses at the rich white folks who put fences up everywhere they wanted to go), that they could be charged with perjury. And they also could be charged as accomplices, although the girl said it had been only the one boy who raped her.

Richard told them who the other boys were, and that they would vouch for him. But the other boys knew, and their parents knew better than them, how it was likely to play out. White girl says she was raped. Black boy says he didn't do it. When his lawyer got them on the stand, they didn't know nothin'. They weren't sure whether Richard was with them all the time or not, just knew that, when they made a run for it, he wasn't there.

When it came time to step up for Richard Slade, everybody stepped back.

Even his own family didn't seem to believe him. Or they just decided to cut their losses. Whatever; by the end of the trial, it was just Philomena. I still remember her sitting there, clutching that ridiculously large purse that was searched meticulously every day by the guards, clinching and unclinching her hands, hoping to exchange a glance with her only child, waiting for the inevitable.

The court-appointed attorney had advised him to forgo a jury trial. The lawyer, who was about two minutes out of law school, told me later, over a few beers and off the record, that he thought a judge would see the irrefutable fact: No one could prove beyond the shadow of a doubt that Richard Slade raped the girl. Hell, there was so much doubt shading that case that you needed a searchlight.

But he hadn't counted on the cops finessing the other boys into going deaf, dumb and blind.

If it had happened a couple of years later, DNA probably would have cleared him, the way it finally, belatedly has now.

Judge Cain chose to believe the girl. I suppose he thought that no one would put herself through a trial like that if she hadn't actually been raped. Or maybe he was hardwired, when it came to black vs. white, to go with white.

She wasn't particularly convincing, but she never wavered. She had been coached well, no doubt. Her parents and older sister sat there every day, hard-eyed, firm-jawed counterparts to Philomena Slade. Alicia looked back at them often for eye contact and, I suppose, reassurance.

When she broke down a couple of times, she only made the accused's lawyer look like a bully. She never really gave a good answer as to why she was at the Quarry at that time of night, just something about "wanting to go for a swim."

Richard Slade got life. When the judge pronounced the verdict, I turned to look at Philomena Slade, but by then, she already had zipped up her sorrow and rage.

Richard himself looked a little gut-shot, the way I would have looked upon receiving a life sentence at the age of seventeen.

They took him away, and not much was heard of Richard Slade, except for his mother's yearly letters to our editorial pages on the date of his conviction, demanding justice. They ran the first one and threw the others away, sometimes sharing them with the newsroom, for the amusement factor. They've done a half-assed mea culpa—or them-a culpa, since we have new Neanderthals doing our deep thinking now—for that "black day for justice" crap four years ago; but being one of our editorial writers apparently means never really having to say you're sorry.

When Mr. DNA entered the picture, people buried forever in black holes started turning up inconveniently innocent. Of course, it was hard to separate the wheat from the chaff, because every murderer and rapist in the federal system wanted some kind of science-based exoneration, but finally it was Slade's turn.

Once they finally were able to compare that long-ago semen with Richard Slade's present-day fluids, it seemed pretty cut-and-dried; but it still took four years and a month to get everyone on board. The commonwealth's attorney, when all hope of keeping Slade in prison legitimately was lost, threw his predecessor to the lions and welcomed Richard Slade back to the land of the living.

Sarah Goodnight is taking all this in as she finishes her fries. "Wow," she says. "This guy must be sorely pissed."

"Funny thing, it didn't seem that way."

Maybe the rage comes later, after the relief wears off. Before it's over, I'm pretty sure the commonwealth will be giving Slade a nice little welcome-home gift, too. I don't know if Marcus Green can make any money for his client and himself suing the girl's family, but he ought to give it his best shot.

We're back in the newsroom by two thirty. It's my day off, but news is news. If I hadn't dragged my ass to court this morning, I know Mark Baer would have been there, poaching my story.

Jackson tells me that Mal Wheelwright wants to see me. It seems wrong, being forced to have a sit-down with our managing editor on a day when I'm not even supposed to be here, but no good deed goes unpunished.

I prefer to stand in Wheelie's office. Makes the meetings go faster.

"So, what're you going to write?"

He ought to know that already, but I explain it to him.

He clears his throat.

"Not too much about our, ah, editorial stance in the past? We don't want to come across looking like the bad guys here."

"Well," I say, yearning to win the lottery so I can tell Wheelie to go fuck himself, "we aren't exactly the good guys."

"That was editorial."

Like the readers give a shit. Anybody who's worked at a paper whose editorial writers have their heads up their asses knows how stupid you look when you say, "It's not me; it's them. Never mind that it comes in the same plastic wrapper. We're news, not editorial."

That usually flies like a concrete block. Like it did with Philomena Slade.

I ease his fears about my further sullying the reputation of this fine rag. It really isn't fair to lay it all on Wheelie, anyhow. He's just following orders. I'd have to go a couple of floors up, to the publisher's office, to find the puppet master who's pulling Wheelie's strings. I can feel the pale fingers of James H. Grubbs all over this one.

So I write the story of Richard Slade, such as I know it.

I tell Sally Velez she's got thirty minutes to read it before I check out. It's almost happy hour, and I could use a couple of pints of happy.

She obliges me, because she knows it's easier to fix any problems the story might have with me sitting beside her, clean and sober. Reaching me later at Penny Lane, as I get happier and happier, can be difficult. Or so I'm told.

"Not bad," she says, after making a couple of changes that I grudgingly admit make it better.

She asks me what happened when the Slades got home, and I have to tell her about my aborted ride. She seems to think it's funny.

She turns to face me.

"What next? Are you going to try to see her?"

"See who?"

She sighs. Sally and I have known each other too long for this kind of bullshit.

"Yeah," I say. "I'm going to give it a shot anyhow. I'll go out there tomorrow, I guess. She'll probably slam the door in my face. I'm getting used to rejection."

CHAPTER THREE

Tuesday

With the exception of three reportedly eventful and unhappy married years, Alicia Parker Simpson lives where she's always lived. When she came back, she didn't even take her husband's name with her.

The geezers at the paper, like Sally and Jackson and Ray Long and me, knew her back when. She worked as an intern one summer, at the publisher's "request." The old publisher, the one before Grubby, lived in the same Windsor Farms neighborhood as the Simpsons. He and Harper Simpson were bourbon buddies.

She wasn't bad. A little brittle, maybe. I doubt if I'd have taken her to a dirt nap the way I did Sarah when she was a cub reporter, but Alicia was a good writer, and she did several freelance features for us after she dropped out of Sweet Briar, before she got tired of journalism. The sense I had: Alicia Parker Simpson got tired very easily. After what she'd been through, the general consensus was that she was entitled to a little fatigue of the soul.

We all knew who she was, of course. After the rape, the paper never mentioned her name, but Richmond isn't that big a town. Everyone handled her with white linen gloves, and maybe that just made her more tired.

Over the years, I've seen her from time to time.

"There she is," someone will whisper, and there she will be. We've even spoken a couple of times. She seems to know me, but maybe that's just good manners.

I ring the bell. Standing here, with the aspirin kicking in finally, in the sunshine and out of the wind, I'm feeling halfway human.

I expect a maid to answer the door. Instead, a West End caricature greets me, although "greet" might not be quite the word I'm looking for.

"Yes?" she says. "May I help you?"

The woman in front of me bears a slight resemblance to Alicia Simpson. I tell her who I am and what I am.

She gives me a firm handshake and identifies herself as Lewis Witt.

I've mercifully never done a stint as society columnist, but Lewis Geneva Simpson Witt I know. Her picture shows up somewhere in our paper every week or so. She must be on every do-good board in the city. And she's Alicia Simpson's older sister.

She invites me inside, then stops me a few steps beyond the door.

"Alicia isn't seeing anyone right now," she explains, planting her athletic body in front of me. I'm guessing she's about fifty, but she looks fine. She looks well-maintained. "I'm sure you can understand. It's been quite a strain on her, with the news media and all. They aren't all as polite as you."

Well, I did put my cigarette out before I knocked and squashed it flat on the stone walkway.

I tell her that I know Alicia from when we worked together at the paper.

Lewis Witt just nods and smiles slightly. I know the smile. It says No Sale.

"Well, do you think Alicia might be willing to talk about it all at a later date?"

"I don't know. You might check back again. But I'm sure you understand this is a very difficult time."

There isn't much left to do, short of getting arrested for trespassing. I give her my card, which she is polite enough not to throw away in front of me, and leave.

As I'm walking back down the slate walkway toward my car, something makes me turn and look back.

In one of the four upstairs windows I can see, Alicia Simpson is standing, the curtains half open. When she realizes I see her, she draws them back.

It can't be a lot of fun. As soon as the DNA evidence told the world that the great Commonwealth of Virginia had stolen twenty-eight years of some innocent black man's life after he was falsely convicted of raping a pampered Windsor Farms teenager, the heat was on.

We've been trying to get an interview ever since, but she has always refused. To Alicia's credit, she did make a statement, in which she said that she was horrified to discover that it was possible an innocent man had been imprisoned on her testimony, but that she was sure, at the time, that she had been right.

"Apparently," her statement concluded, "I was wrong."

In the past four years, she's never been unpleasant to the occasional reporter who manages to waylay her when she makes what seem to be more and more infrequent forays out of her home. But she's usually with someone else, and that someone else usually whisks her away before she can be bothered.

After Richard Slade got the long-awaited writ of actual innocence, she issued another statement, apologizing for her long-ago mistake and wishing the alleged rapist well. For right now, it seems that's all the fourth estate is going to get out of Alicia Parker Simpson.

I have time to run back to my apartment and grab a quick bite before my real workday begins. Kate is still letting me rent from her, which I appreciate. I have come to think of the Prestwould as home. Most of the other residents are older than me, and most of them surely have bigger stock portfolios, but we get along. And in how many places can a fifty-something newspaper reporter be referred to on a regular basis as "young man"?

Custalow is taking his lunch break. He's sitting there at the table, looking out at the park six floors below, munching on one of the two peanut-butter-and-jelly sandwiches he's made for himself.

"The hawk's back," he says. I walk closer to the window and see the red-tailed hawk that keeps the pigeon and squirrel population manageable. This time of year, you can spot him a mile away, a fat silhouette adorning the top of an oak tree like an ornament left over from Christmas.

I observe that the radiators are making more noise than usual. Custalow glares at me like I've questioned his janitorial competence.

"We're working on it," he says and tucks into the other sandwich.

It works out pretty well. Abe Custalow has a roof over his head and something resembling a salary. I have an old friend to help me make the rent payment to my ex-wife.

"Oh," he says, "Clara Westbrook was looking for you."

Clara probably needs a light bulb replaced. Or just some company. The grande dame of the Prestwould is a social butterfly, and her friends keep leaving for "independent living" or the Great Beyond.

"So Slade is finally free?"

"Seems like it."

Abe finishes the second sandwich and wipes his mouth with the back of his hand.

"Good."

Abe Custalow has spent some time as a guest of the state, and it has occurred to me that he might have crossed paths with Richard Slade. I've never asked him. Prison isn't something he really likes to talk about. I doubt he'll want it mentioned in his obituary.

Still, since he brought it up . . .

"Did you know him?"

He looks at me.

"Yeah, a little."

And then he gets up, takes his paper plate into the kitchen, and is out the back door leading from the kitchen to the service hallway before I can ask him anything else.

The place still looks good, despite my and Custalow's best efforts to turn it into a bachelor pigsty. Since Kate owns it, she has a key. She is prone to drop by from time to time, just to make sure I'm not smoking indoors or piling used Miller High Life cans in the living room. When we were married, she was as big a slob as me, but now that she's a landlady, she takes her job seriously.

Still, the rent's reasonable, especially with Custalow's modest contribution. If I had to pay what my neighbors do, or bear the full brunt of that four-figure monthly condo fee, I'd be gone by sundown.

I have time to take a twenty-minute power nap and then check in with Clara before work.

When I get there and knock, she yells down the hallway for me to come on in. Clara doesn't believe in locking her door, even after the little theft ring that Custalow broke up last year, resulting in his co-worker going to jail and him becoming our Head Janitor in Charge.

Clara's got some health issues, but she's not complaining. She drags that oxygen bottle behind her in its little wagon like a pet and offers to get me something to eat or drink. I tell her I know where the bourbon is, but that my boss likes it if he doesn't smell liquor on my breath, at least not before sundown.

"Nobody has any fun anymore," she says.

She's right about that. Gone are the days of the two-bourbon lunch and the sleepy afternoons. And it's hard to disappear for long when the editors have your cellphone number.

I fix her a very light Scotch and, what the hell, make one for myself, too.

Clara says she invited me up to ask if I want the leftover booze from her New Year's Eve party, which I and seemingly half of Richmond attended. Clara planted herself at the end of the big foyer leading into the living room and greeted everyone with a kiss. I stopped by for a while, and she whispered to me when I left, "If I've got to go, I want to go wearing a party dress."

I thank her for the offer and tell her I've got a fairly ample supply of both the brown and white liquors.

"Well," she says, with the twinkle in her eye that'll be the last thing she loses, "you go through it pretty fast."

We chat for a couple of minutes, then she says what probably was on her mind from the start.

"Wasn't that awful about Alicia Parker Simpson?"

I observe that it was pretty awful about Richard Slade, too. I'd take feeling guilty over twenty-eight years in prison any day.

She waves her hand as if swatting away a tiresome fly.

"Oh, you know what I mean. The whole thing."

I mention knowing the woman briefly and then tell Clara about my abbreviated ride with the Slade family.

"I can't blame her," she says. "She was his mother. I read about how hard she fought, all those years. That's what a mother does."

She takes a sip, trying to make the one drink she knows should be her limit last as long as possible.

"I knew her parents."

Clara probably could say that about just about anyone in the West End, where "Who was your family?" is not considered to be a rude or inconsequential question.

I glance at my watch. Since I worked gratis yesterday, I think the paper can afford to spot me a few minutes today.

"Tell me," I say, taking a seat on the ottoman facing her.

Harper Simpson, long since taken from us by a heart attack suffered in the bathroom at the Commonwealth Club, was a well-compensated corporate lawyer. His family had made its money, as had so many in Richmond, in tobacco, and the family still seems to be living off that long-ago bounty.

"At least," Clara says, "I don't hear about Alicia having to work, and Wesley and Lewis certainly don't, although Lewis at least married pretty well."

I tell her I met Lewis Simpson Witt earlier today, and that she seemed to be quite the brick.

"Oh, she's a tough cookie," Clara agrees.

Clara, well into her eighties, had been a contemporary of Harper and Simone Simpson.

"They were very glamorous," she said, taking another small sip. "And their kids were, too."

It isn't that hard to imagine Lewis as the young, raven-haired beauty Clara describes, even if she has, like the rest of us, collected a few wrinkles and pounds along the way.

She was a debutante and went to what was then Randolph-Macon Woman's College. She was the kind of girl who always made her parents proud.

"She would have been a beauty queen," Clara says, "but Harper thought beauty pageants were trashy. I remember they had a terrible fight about it one year. But she always gave way to Harper. I tried to convince him one time that she wouldn't automatically turn into a red-light girl if she got picked as Miss Richmond."

Clara was runner-up for Miss Virginia back in the day, although you'd never find that out from her. So I could imagine her intervening on Lewis's behalf, to no avail.

"Harper was a good man, but he was stubborn," she says, and takes another sip.

"But it seemed like they got, you know, diminishing returns with those kids. The other two started out like Lewis, the apple of everybody's eye. Wes and Alicia were adorable. Everybody said so, not just me."

I ask her if she thought it was the rape that changed her.

Clara thinks about it a minute. I try not to hear her breathing with the help of her little friend.

"No," she says. "I think there was something odd about her before that. She had a way of zoning out. You'd be talking to her, and then you'd see that she wasn't really there.

"And, by then, they were already having trouble with Wesley."

Coming from the West End, where girls wind up with androgynous, family-heirloom names as often as not, Wesley could have been the third sister.

"Oh, no," Clara says, laughing. "Wesley was all boy. He was the apple of Harper and Simone's eyes. Before he . . . well, before he lost his mind, I suppose you'd say."

He was fifteen, a straight-A student and already a starter on the lacrosse team as a freshman, popular and handsome.

"And then, he came home from school one day and told them he couldn't go back. Just like that."

Clara snaps her fingers.

"He went to a 'special' school somewhere up in the valley, and then he came back and lived with them, but from then on, he was in and out of different kinds of homes. I saw him at Simone's funeral, last year, and I meant to speak to him, if he even still knows me. But then he disappeared. I suppose Lewis and her husband look after him now, if anybody does."

Clara shakes her head. I need to go, just to keep her from talking. It's pretty obvious that the oxygen tank is having trouble keeping up.

"I always felt bad about it all, felt bad that I couldn't help Wesley in some way. You know, I was his godmother."

I have one hand on the ottoman to push myself up when she says it. I stop.

"Oh, I know," Clara says, laughing and wheezing a little. "I buried my lede."

Clara never forgets anything, including old newspaper jargon. I told her about burying ledes one time when she'd spun some fifteen-minute yarn about a run-down home she was trying to help save near the VCU campus before finally mentioning that she and her late husband had reared three kids there.

"I've left him something in my will. Maybe it'll keep him independent for a few more years."

But after that day when he told them he couldn't go back to school, Clara rarely ever saw him.

"I think there was some sense of shame. They diagnosed it as schizophrenia, but neither Harper nor Simone would talk about it, even with me. They'd just change the subject, and after a while, you just stopped asking. And I never tried as hard as I might have to stay in touch with him, later."

The general feeling, Clara said, was that "losing" his beloved son, and then the rape of his youngest daughter three years later, contributed greatly to Harper Simpson's fatal heart attack when he wasn't yet sixty.

"That's all hooey, of course. What caused Harper Simpson's heart to quit was too much Smithfield ham and too many Marlboros."

I make sure she's OK and take my leave.

"Come back anytime," she says, walking me slowly to the door, which only wears her out and delays my parting a couple of minutes.

Feldman, a.k.a. Mr. McGrumpy, the Prestwould's resident busy-body (although he has plenty of competition), is in the lobby when I come down.

"Ah," he says, "and how is Clara today?"

He loves to do that shit. He saw the elevator go up to twelve and then come down, depositing me in the lobby. The only other unit on twelve is unoccupied.

I tell him she's fine and congratulate him on his skills as a snoop. I'd like to throttle him sometimes, but he's almost as old as Clara, and I think they put you in jail for dough-popping people that age, even if they do deserve it.

"And how is our resident felon?"

He must spend half his waking hours down here in the lobby, watching and waiting for chances to piss people off.

He's really pushing it. If McGrumpy had his way, Custalow would be back out on the street. Other than one rather unfortunate and semi-deserved killing, Abe Custalow is as gentle as a lamb; but I think McGrumpy's afraid our maintenance man and my co-tenant might pinch his head off and shit down his neck, and I like the idea of the old bastard being a little jumpy.

"Abe was looking for you," I tell him as I leave.

CHAPTER FOUR

Saturday

The forecast is for snow. Sitting in the den and looking out, I think the TV moron with the bad hair might have gotten it right. Even a blind hog finds an acorn now and then.

One of the disadvantages of living ten blocks from the paper is that you can't exactly claim the roads are too icy. I tried it once, told Jackson I might fall on those slick brick sidewalks and hurt myself. He reminded me that the bus stops right in front of my building.

When the phone rings, I let the answering machine pick it up. That's only fair. I wouldn't even be up now if I could have gone back to sleep after I got my acid reflux wakeup call at five.

Then I hear Sally Velez's voice, and it doesn't sound like a casual call. What call is casual at seven thirty on a Saturday morning?

"Alicia Simpson has been shot. They don't think she's going to make it."

I pick up and ask her where.

"Somewhere on West Cary. She's at MCV."

"When?"

"It must've just happened. Maybe an hour or two ago. Some friend of Ray Long's, an ER nurse, called him and he called me. I don't know much else."

"We're sure it's her?"

"Pretty sure. Sure enough that I'm calling you."

Point taken. Unlike some editors, Sally doesn't get her kicks by playing newspaper. When she pulls the alarm, there's probably a fire.

I put down my coffee and head for the bedroom. There on the floor, where I left them, are my pants and shirt. I can always take a shower later and get presentable before I start my real workday, the part I get paid for.

I see Custalow in the lobby, talking to Marcia the manager. I tell him what's going on.

He shakes his head.

"You didn't get in until one thirty."

I tell him I'll get the hours back sometime.

"After you're dead," he says, and turns back to Marcia, to whom he is trying to explain the latest plumbing issue.

I light a Camel while I'm on the front steps. I'm not dressed for bad weather, and I debate for a few seconds whether I should go back up. But then I'd have to waste a cigarette. Screw it.

The air is cold and still, and it seems like I can already feel the snow. But when I get to the car, there's no evidence of ice on my windshield, just an empty Bud on the hood, which some young scholar must have mistaken for a recycling bin sometime after I got in. I think briefly of the Black family's current contribution to higher education. I need to give Andi a call.

The VCU hospital is a long walk or a short drive from the Prestwould. Everyone beyond a certain age still calls it MCV, as in Medical College of Virginia.

With HIPAA and all, it's very difficult to get information out of hospitals these days, or at least it is supposed to be. I recognize one of the receptionists, though. As luck would have it, she's Goat Johnson's niece. I've known her since she was a baby.

"Willie," she says, brightening when she sees me. "You look like you've been run over by a bus. Sure you don't need the emergency room entrance?"

I tell her what's happened. She looks around and then gives me what I need.

Alicia Parker Simpson is in intensive care. I can't get in there without a pass, and even Goat Johnson's niece can't do that for me.

"You can go up to the floor, though," she says, "and maybe go to the family waiting room."

I thank her and ask her when Goat's going to be back in town.

"Ah," she says, "he's too big for Oregon Hill now. I think he's high-hatting us."

"Hard to believe a guy named Goat could high-hat anybody, even if he is a college president."

She laughs and sends me on my way.

It isn't that easy finding the family room. I've never been in a big hospital yet that wasn't designed along the same lines as those corn mazes every farmer these days seems to create for the city folk to get lost in. By the time I reach my destination, I have met the same dazed-looking older couple twice. I want to help them, but I can barely help myself.

The family room is the kind of place you never want to be unless you must. Everybody in there has a loved one, or at least a relative, hanging by a thread. The fear and despair are as thick as a river-bottom fog. Teaching hospitals are where they send you when nothing less can possibly save you; and ICUs in teaching hospitals are where skill has to turn the wheel over to luck and prayer, and the prayers don't get answered on anything like a regular basis.

When I walk in, the first person I see is Carl Witt. I recognize Lewis Witt's husband from his photographs, which regularly adorn the paper's pages, either for his work as an attorney or with Lewis on his arm at some fundraiser.

He's sitting forward, his elbows resting on his thighs and his hands clasped together. He seems to be dozing, but then he looks up at me, and I see that he's wide awake.

"Yes?" he says. He can see that I'm not a doctor. The way I'm dressed, he might think I'm one of the neighborhood's homeless who wander in occasionally, looking for free medical attention or just warmth.

"I heard about Alicia," I say. "I used to work with her." Well, that's not technically a lie.

"Where?"

At the paper, I tell him.

The nickel drops.

"Ah," he says. "You guys don't waste much time, do you?"

I say nothing. Somebody with a family member headed for the light doesn't really care to hear about the public's right to know. Anyhow, this story probably is more about the public's thirst for information it doesn't really need, a.k.a. entertainment. And we are entertainment's eager little handmaidens.

He sighs.

"Well," he says, "everybody's got a job to do."

Witt, being a corporate lawyer, understands how it feels to be a notch or two below whale shit in the public's pecking order. But at least corporate lawyers get paid pretty well. I once asked Kate why she didn't go for the money instead of trying to change the world through our criminal justice system.

She asked me why I turned down that PR job they offered me at Philip Morris, since I was pretty much single-handedly propping up the tobacco industry anyhow.

"You could get some of your cigarette money back," she said.

I told her that even scum-sucking, Commie journalists like me had their standards.

Carl Witt is willing, once we've gotten past our opening parry, to tell as much as he knows about "the incident."

"Alicia gets up every morning and goes to work out. God knows why. She weighs about ninety damn pounds. But she gets to that gym on West Main by five thirty, and she's out by seven. She says it's pretty empty that time of day."

They found her car, with the engine running, rammed into a parking meter just beyond the stoplight where West Cary crosses Meadow. A city cop came by and saw that the driver was slumped over the steering wheel. He thought he might have a case of severely drunk driving on his hands, but then he saw that the side window was shot out. And then he saw all the blood.

"They told Lewis that the rescue squad was there in less than ten minutes, but I don't know if there was much they could do. Lewis is back there now. They're not supposed to let anybody in, but you know Lewis. Or I guess you don't."

"We've met."

We sit there quietly for maybe ten minutes, and then Lewis Witt comes out. She hasn't had time to do what you do when you're fifty and want to get your game face on before you meet the world. Her mouth is a grim, tight line.

"She's gone."

Her husband gets up and embraces her. There are others in the room, strangers with their own grief. She looks over her husband's shoulder and sees me.

"Who are you?" she asks me, in a surprisingly strong voice. And then she remembers.

"You're that reporter," she says. "Get out."

Nobody seems to have much use for journalists invading their most private moments these days. Go figure.

I express my sympathy as I back out the door. I really mean it. What I remember about Alicia Simpson is almost all good. She was a competent writer who was not averse to the concept that someone else might know something about the craft that she didn't. She was a little fragile, I thought, a little too jumpy to be a good newspaper reporter. But she was blessed with enough family money that she never had to find that out.

Whatever happened that night at the Quarry, twenty-eight years ago, I'll never know, but both Alicia Simpson and Richard Slade definitely were the worse for it.

Back at the paper, I blog a few paragraphs so our potential readers don't have to actually buy the Sunday paper. I try to leave something really juicy out of the blogs to tease them ("Tune in to the Sunday paper, folks, for the full story"), but the circulation numbers tell me that's not working so well.

My cellphone rings. It really does ring, like a damn phone is supposed to. What is so cool about having your phone play "Billy

Jean" or "Stairway to Heaven"? It's like that singing fish thing that was so big a few years back. Funny once, maybe twice, then you just want to shoot it.

It's Peggy.

"He's gone again."

Les. This happens now and then, and I usually know where to look.

I tell her I'll be there in half an hour. I have a couple of hours before I'm expected at the paper.

Les Hacker, the light of my addled mother's life and the guy who saved my butt from being barbecued last year, has gone walking.

We haven't had to get him off the roof lately, but he is prone to occasionally wandering off. Les's body is still in pretty good shape. The last time I got the cops to find him, he was all the way out of town, headed toward Williamsburg. When they stopped him, they said he looked confused, like somebody who's just woke up from a dream.

He reminds me of a comedy bit I heard once: "Grandma's walking five miles a day now, and we have no idea where she is."

I always try to find him myself first. I start in the neighborhood, then expand my search into Blackwell and the Fan. I don't want social services coming over and telling Peggy she's got to put him in some damn home.

When my mother opens the front door, I am temporarily overwhelmed by the sweet smell of wacky weed, but Peggy seems relatively coherent. The day is young.

"He was right here," she says, "watching that ESPN. I went to do the dishes and then took a shower, and when I got back, he was gone."

This time, it's easy. I look in their bedroom closet and see that the old catcher's mitt, remnant of his last pro baseball stop with the Richmond V's, is missing.

So, I get in my ancient but indestructible Honda and head toward The Diamond. It's been more than twenty years since they demolished Parker Field, where Les once played, and built something with a newer, more hip name (even if the damn thing is falling down now). Hey, I'm no mossback, but things have to change names for about fifty years before I really buy in. Holding back the hands of time, one of our younger reporters told me once, when I was ranting about texting and tweeting, is a twenty-four-hour-a-day job.

Sure enough, I find Les, walking up Boulevard, just past Buzz and Ned's. I manage to pull over and park a block ahead of him and intercept him as he's walking past, that 500-yard stare telling me he thinks he's late for the game. I notice the first few snowflakes. Les has on a light sweater.

"Hey, Les," I ask him, like I'd just happened to bump into him there, "where you going?"

He doesn't seem to recognize me for about five seconds. Then he wakes up and looks around him.

"I did it again, didn't I?" he asks me. He looks as abashed as a kid who's just wet the bed.

"Big game today?" I asked him. He looks down at the mitt he's carrying in his right hand, and we both laugh.

He looks around and figures out where he is.

"Can we get in the car?" he says finally. "It's cold as a witch's tit out here."

I bring him home. I can see Peggy's neighbor, Jerry Cannady, looking at us out his front window. Jerry no doubt knows what's happened. He's always complaining about something Les has done, none of which has ever harmed another human being, to my knowledge. I give Jerry the finger, and the blinds snap shut.

Peggy calls Les an old fool, asks rhetorically what she's going to do with him, then hugs him.

I stay around for a few minutes and let Peggy fix me a baloney sandwich.

I ask her about her erstwhile tenant, the redoubtable Awesome Dude.

"Oh," she says, "he went walking a couple of days ago. He'll be back."

The Dude, saved by Peggy from a life of homeless shelters, park benches and lean-to's by the river, occasionally still hears the call of the wild.

I note that her men seem to be prone to running away.

"Go fuck yourself," she explains. In Peggy-speak, "Go fuck yourself" translates as "Let's change the subject."

I ask her if that's the same mouth she used to kiss me goodnight with.

"I never kissed you goodnight," she says, laughing. "You were too ugly."

"Did you hear about that Windsor Farms girl?" she asks me. I'm thinking, shit, the TV guys have got it, too. Usually, it would take a nuclear blast to wake them up on Saturdays, when the whole crew of most of our local stations seems to consist of VCU mass com students with good hair and empty heads. They probably got it from my blog. Talk about red meat for the on-the-airheads: Rich, blonde former debutante shot to death at a stoplight five days after the man she accused of raping her gets his "writ of actual innocence."

I tell Peggy about my day so far.

"I guess it isn't going to be hard to come up with a suspect," Peggy says. "That poor boy. After all he's been through."

Well, I suggest, it does seem as if Richard Slade might be a logical choice. If I'd just gotten back from twenty-eight years in the big house for a crime I apparently didn't commit, I might have built up a slight case of resentment. I mean, just how many people in the city of Richmond did have a reason to shoot Alicia Parker Simpson twice in the face on her way to her morning workout?

Peggy shakes her head.

"That whole thing, even back then, seemed so bogus. I never did believe Philomena's boy would've done that."

I have half a sandwich in my mouth and have trouble speaking until I wash it down.

"Wait. What? You know Philomena Slade?"

Peggy wipes her hands on a paper napkin.

"Well, she was Philomena Lee back then."

I implore Peggy to tell me more. She has to circle around it. Eventually, though, I find out that Richard Slade is probably my second cousin.

CHAPTER FIVE

Sunday

There's about an inch of snow on the ground, but the sun's out now. Andi and I are headed down to Millie's for brunch. I haven't seen my daughter since Christmas. She gave me a tie and a fifth of Jack Black, which she probably got for next to nothing at her most recent stop in her apparent quest to wait tables at every restaurant and bar in the city limits. I gave her cash. That's what she said she wanted, but it didn't seem to thrill her that much.

Andi probably will graduate from VCU about the same time she checks the last eatery in town off her to-do list. Like the tortoise, her progress is slow but steady, a course or two a semester. I hope that, like the tortoise, she crosses the finish line one day.

As we make our way across town through the slush, my mind is still reeling a bit from Peggy's latest bombshell.

"Why didn't you tell me about this before?" I asked after I'd finally dragged it out of her. Peggy has never had much of a filter between her brain and her mouth. She thinks it, she says it.

"It wasn't any of your business."

I told her that it sure as hell was my business, but she crossed her arms like some sulking little kid and told me to change the subject or get out.

It isn't exactly a big deal anymore to be of "mixed race." Mixing the races might be the only thing that can save these Benighted States of America, although I'm sure we'd find some other reason to hate each other.

Artie Lee, saxophonist and bon vivant, died when he wrapped a car around a sycamore tree while I was still crawling. I inherited almost none of his light-skinned African-American physical characteristics. Growing up in Oregon Hill, which was as white as Minute Rice back then, that was probably just as well.

I can vaguely remember Peggy taking me over a couple of times to visit a black family in Highland Springs, when I was still pre-school age.

The family, it turns out, was the Lees.

You know the Hillary Clinton thing about it taking a village? Well, the Lees were a small town, everybody looking out for everyone else's kids, everybody closing ranks around their weakest, sharing what they could. Kind of like America is supposed to be.

And one of Artie Lee's first cousins was Philomena, who was twelve or thirteen when Peggy began "seeing" Artie.

"She was so bright, so sweet," Peggy said, before she refused to say any more. "She used to take care of the younger ones, like she was their momma."

Philomena and Peggy kept in touch for a while, and Peggy said the late Artie's cousin once even ventured over to visit her in Oregon Hill.

"But she said people were giving her the evil eye, and she didn't come back."

Peggy said she hadn't seen Philomena since probably 1980.

"When her son was arrested, maybe three years after that, somebody else answered the phone, and said she'd moved. And I never tried to get up with her again.

"But I just know Philomena Lee wouldn't have raised a boy that would rape a girl like that. He was—is—her only child, too. Don't know what happened to the daddy."

A lot of that going around, I want to say.

In adulthood, I have never tried to run away from my heritage, but back then, when I was a kid, it was easier to be "us" than to be "them." My friends knew, and some of my enemies suspected and, it being the South, fights ensued. It was easier to just let people think I was something exotic without any of that old Dixie baggage attached.

Sometimes, though, the truth will out no matter how hard you try to bottle it up. Faulkner was right about the past. You can drive a stake through the son-of-a-bitch's heart, bury it deep, and it'll still rise up waving the Stars and Bars.

I checked around last night, and my best cops' source, the redoubtable Peachy Love, told me that they were already questioning Richard Slade about his whereabouts early yesterday morning. He said he was at home asleep, and Philomena backed him up.

"But she's his mother," Peachy said. "It's just a matter of time." She's probably right.

I am obliged to take another crack at Philomena Slade. Maybe, with my genealogy brought up to date, she will cut me some slack if I play the family card. The white sheep returns.

We have a great meal at Millie's, as always. We both prefer its frantic, pants-on-fire ambience and heartburn specials to the somnolent brunch buffets at the Jefferson.

We at least have Millie's in common.

I ask her how school's going, and she reminds me that the spring semester hasn't started yet.

"Well, then, how'd you do in the fall?"

"I did OK."

I ask her if she might be able to expand a little on "OK." Back in my college days, I remind her, when the earth's crust was still warm, they actually defined a student's progress with certain letters: A, B, C and such.

Her grades come directly to her. That's the way they do it now. The student is an adult, albeit one whose parents are writing the checks, and it would be an offense against the student's privacy and dignity to send Mom and Dad any information as to what the second mortgage is actually yielding, education-wise.

Andi's a good kid, though, and I know she does appreciate my belated effort at parenthood. I missed most of the diaper-changing and wasn't around for toilet training, so I'm trying to pay off my guilt with tuition and fees. Her mother and stepfather have enough bills to pay, and their two boys are fast approaching college age themselves.

"I got an A in English and a B in psych," she says. I do the math in my head and figure she might be above C-level overall by now.

I ask her about the third course. She was very pumped, I seem to remember, about getting into this "very cool" course in African-American history.

She frowns.

"I dropped it, back in November. I thought I told you."

She probably did.

"How come?"

"I didn't feel welcome," she says, after a short pause. "I was the only white kid in there. I felt, you know, like it was all on me. Every time they'd talk about Nat Turner, or segregation or something, I felt like everybody was giving me the fish-eye."

Andi knows next to nothing about Peggy's side of her family, just that her grandfather on her dad's side died a long time ago. Jeanette's never told her, and neither have I. Am I a racist? Doesn't feel that way, but somehow Andi and I have never had that talk, the one where she finds out that she has more of a stake in African-American history than she knows.

She'd think it was "cool" to be something other than blue-collar, white-bread Scots-Irish. But telling her now would also entail tacitly admitting that I hadn't told her for almost twenty-two years. It's complicated. Maybe I've been too hard on Peggy.

"So," I ask, slipping very gingerly into these shark-infested waters, "how are you . . . where are you . . . ?"

"When am I going to graduate?"

I nod my head, grateful that I haven't upset the delicate balance of this father-daughter get-together by asking an indelicate question.

"If everything goes right, I should be through in a couple of years, maybe spring of 2013."

Well, I say, that's not so bad, thinking to myself how seldom everything goes right.

"You know," she says, reaching across the table and laying one of her hands over mine, "we don't have to do this. I'm making pretty good money. I can support myself. I don't need a degree."

I shake my head.

"No, sweetie. One day, trust me, a college degree's going to be the difference. There'll be a job somewhere, probably one that doesn't relate to anything you're studying. You'll really want it, but the human resources assholes will decree that 'the applicant must have an undergraduate degree,' and some jerk with some bullshit major like psychology will get it instead of you."

"Dad," she says, "I'm probably going to major in psych."

Oh yeah.

"Well," she says, as we slide out of our booth and head toward the door, "maybe you're right, but the world's changing. It isn't all about the BA or BS anymore."

The world is changing, I tell her, but there always will be a premium on people who prove they can stay the course.

I turn to her when I hear her snort.

"What?"

"Says the man with three ex-wives."

As we walk past the bar, I see a guy sitting there reading the Sunday paper, with my story across the top of A1. ALICIA SIMPSON SHOT TO DEATH. They had a hard time with the headline, I'm sure. Who was Alicia Simpson? Former rape victim? Rape alleger? Misidentifier?

I wonder how deep the cops are into Richard and Philomena Slade's shit already.

I ask Andi if she'd like to take a short trip to Richmond's most exclusive club.

"You're taking me to the Country Club of Virginia?"

"Much better than that."

I tell her a little about the Philadelphia Quarry on the way there—how it had been around since the 1930s, how the stone they cut out of there went to, duh, Philadelphia, where I guess they built something with it. Andi stifles her yawns.

The Quarry's secret membership list probably has always included a Prestwouldian or two. Some are shareholders. Some, like Clara Westbrook, are "summer members," invited from year to year at the pleasure of the shareholders.

When she first took Kate and me over as her guests, I could see my beaming bride's eyes light up. Nothing turned my third wife on like the prospect of breaking into some club. *Someday,* the thought balloon above her head said, *they'll ask me.*

As Kate pumped Clara for more details about the place, I chose not to tell either of them that I'd already been to the Quarry, several times and uninvited.

All the Oregon Hill boys knew the Quarry. It was almost a rite of passage to sneak into this place where only what we thought of as rich people were allowed. There was always a way to get around or through the fence, and nothing was more delicious on a hot summer night than skinny-dipping and pissing in the deep, clear, cold water of the well-to-do. We'd go over there from the Hill after midnight when we were old enough to drive and could get a car—me, Abe, McGonnigal, Goat Johnson, Andy Peroni, John Wesley Samms. Unlike Richard Slade, we never got caught, but it was close a couple of times.

Alicia Parker Simpson's rape gave the place the kind of notoriety its members would've paid dearly to avoid, but since the trial in 1984, it has slipped back into welcome obscurity. The Quarry has been on my mind ever since Richard Slade's release from prison brought it back to the surface.

We drive through the city, taking one detour so I can see the spot where Alicia met her demise. Yellow police tape surrounds the spot, and a handful of black kids have drifted over from the convenience store across the street to gawk.

Once we get to Carytown, we take McCoy Street south, go past City Stadium and then over the expressway, and we're in Windsor Farms. Coming this way, it seems like we should have to show our passports. It's another world, the green, green grass of old money.

I get lost once. Then, suddenly, we're there. My intention was to find the place, show it to Andi through the barbed-wire fence, tell her a few stories about my misspent youth and be on our way.

But the gate to the parking lot is open, although it's four months and forty degrees from swimming weather.

I drive in and see that some kind of maintenance crew is there. Two old guys in jeans and jackets are getting ready to paint one of the sheds. I guess they think we're members, because they leave us alone.

"What is this place?" Andi asks. Like most people in Richmond, she's never seen it.

I tell her that it is an icon of my wayward youth.

"Also, it's where Alicia Parker Simpson was raped."

I fill her in, and we take a short walk around the place.

Like almost everything except my damn waistline, the Quarry seems to have shrunk over the years. I remember it being much bigger. There's a white sandy beach with some picnic tables. Beyond that is the water, with a fifty-foot wall of granite behind it. The Quarry is shaped like an S, with the tails at either end just out of view.

The two sheds are still there, one of them still housing the men's and women's changing rooms. The buildings are nondescript cinder block.

I walk into the men's room there, where Alicia Parker Simpson's and Richard Slade's lives changed so long ago. The bare smell of concrete and mildew make it seem more like a YMCA summer camp than a den of exclusivity.

"This is like the most hoity-toity club in Richmond? It smells."

Andi is behind me. She is obviously unimpressed. I tell her the story that brought me here, and I tell her how we used to sneak in.

"Seems like sneaking into a pay toilet," she says before she goes outside.

The bare sycamores hover over us. Their dead leaves float on the greenish surface. A lone heron flies over, headed for the river that's just beyond the cliff we're facing.

"Well," I tell Andi, "it was much bigger when I was a boy."

"Wasn't everything?" she asks.

"Yes," I reply, "it was."

"So," she says, "this was where that black guy was supposed to have raped the white girl way back when, and she's the one that got killed yesterday?"

"Yeah. That's pretty much it."

"Wow. Sucks being him today."

I drop her off at her apartment on Floyd, the one she shares with another girl and two guys. They're just friends, she told me the first time I came by. Not, I'm hoping, friends with benefits.

I shouldn't stop by the paper. It is my day off. But my car seems to have a magnet in it, guiding me to one of the empty parking spaces beside the building. Even on weekdays, there are often empty spaces right out front. In its infinite wisdom, the company that owns us built its corporate headquarters right across the street from the newspaper building, back when newspapers made money. Now, you could fit all the suits and the worker bees in one of the two buildings, but nobody's done that. I guess it would be kind of like running up the white flag.

I stop by and say hello to Enos Jackson on the copy desk, where he seems at least moderately content to end his working career. Jackson gets grumpy sometimes. He's done bigger things than this. But he knows he's lucky to have a job at all.

I see Sarah Goodnight's head barely visible over the top of her computer terminal. She seems to be the only reporter in the place.

"Oh," she says when she sees me standing there. "Hi. Just trying to finish my latest Pulitzer nominee. It's about catfish."

Something—could be global warming or the fertilizer that gets washed into the James upstream—is making our catfish grow to monstrous proportions. A couple have topped 100 pounds. They look like fish versions of the overweight, Big Gulp-sucking kids I see around town. Maybe the catfish are going to McDonald's. And Sarah, the weekend reporter, has been elected to go down to the docks and interview some of the people who catch them for food. You're only supposed to eat them a couple of times a month, the health officials say. The river is still recovering from about a century of industrial abuse.

Two things: If you're desperate enough to look on river catfish as a reliable source of protein, you're going to eat what you catch—all of what you catch. And, anything that you should eat only once or twice a month, you probably shouldn't eat at all. A little bit of cancer is a little too much.

I read Sarah's story. She's done the best she can, even got some pretty good quotes from a couple of the old black men and women fishing down there. She found out that most of them, including the ones going out into the deep current in leaky rowboats, can't swim a lick.

"Honey," she quotes one woman as saying, a grandmother with her five-year-old grandson at her side, "something's gonna get you."

Chuck Apple, who does night cops on Sundays and Mondays, comes in from a shooting. No fatalities this time, so it's maybe a 1-2-18 on B5. I ask him what's happening on the Alicia Simpson front.

"The cops say they'll have an announcement tomorrow morning, nine A.M."

They don't tell you ahead of time that they're having a press conference unless there's some good news—at least their version of good news, which means they've got their man, or will sometime soon.

Chuck isn't what you'd call extremely motivated. He's having to take a couple of unpaid furlough days, like the rest of the workers, and I know he's worked at least one of those, because, as he said, somebody's got to put the damn paper out. But he's not exactly gung-ho. Five years ago, he might be out there hitting up every source he knows, trying to find out what the police are planning to trot out for their dog-and-pony show tomorrow.

Hell, we both have a pretty good idea of what's coming, although it would have been good to have nailed it down. It's always satisfying to a cops reporter to know the police chief is spitting out his cornflakes, reading his day's itinerary in his morning paper.

"Can't be but one thing," Apple says.

I nod. Like Andi said, it sucks being Richard Slade.

CHAPTER SIX

Monday

Why can't they ever have press conferences in the afternoon, or at least on a day when I'm paid to work? I don't have to be here, but if it wasn't me, it'd be Mark Baer or Handley Pace or some other byline poacher half my age. It's my story, even if it is my day off.

When I get to city hall, damned if Baer isn't the first person I see, all spiffy and ready for an easy A1 byline to add to the résumé he still hopes he can convert into a job at the *Washington Post*.

"I thought this was your day off," he says.

I tell him to get the fuck out of there, and he does.

There are only six of us there—me, some freelancer from the local entertainment weekly and four TV types. The *Post* hasn't deigned to send somebody down. We're outnumbered by the cops, which seems to piss L. D. Jones off. He shoots me a death-ray glare. He's still harboring grudges from last year, when my "interference in police matters" led to the uncomfortable revelation that one of his lieutenants was a murderer.

"No smoking," the chief says, looking at me.

We're outside, for Christ's sake, in front of City Hall, freezing our butts off. Am I going to give the birds cancer? But I don't need any more trouble from L. D. Jones. I stub out my Camel. He's still glaring at me. I reach down, pick it up and walk fifty feet to the nearest trash can. The chief says something to the flunky next to him. They laugh.

There is little news here that a four-year-old couldn't have figured out. You free a man on Monday after he's done twenty-eight years for a rape he didn't commit, and then the woman who accused him gets shot through the head on Saturday. One plus one equals two. Richard Slade is back behind bars. They got him yesterday. He had six days of open windows and doors that locked from the inside.

The mayor's there, too, to reassure the people of Richmond that he personally won't let innocent people get shot to death in their cars. Well, he won't let folks from Windsor Farms get shot that way, anyhow. He's probably the one who insisted we do it outside, with City Hall as the backdrop. He must have laryngitis, though, because he lets the chief do the talking. In good health, Hizzoner would only relinquish a microphone when you tore it from his cold, dead hands.

Jones is asked if they're sure they have the right man.

"We, ah, can't go into that right now," the chief says, "but we have strong evidence pointing to the suspect."

"Do you have the murder weapon?"

Jesus. Whoever shot Alicia Simpson threw the weapon down on Cary Street, which is where the cops found it. No prints. No serial number. It was in the paper, dumb-ass. Can TV reporters not read?

He's never going to call on me, so I yell it out, loud enough so he has to answer.

"Do you have forensic evidence of any type linking Richard Slade to Alicia Simpson's murder?"

The chief would really like to pistol-whip me. He takes a deep breath. He seems to be counting.

"We can't reveal that information at the present time," he says, then adds, "but I'm sure we will have a breakthrough there very soon."

In other words, no.

The TV types were hoping for a perp walk, but they're disappointed. Slade is already in the city lockup, and they have at least spared him the usual public shaming, for now.

The press conference lasts all of fifteen minutes. Nothing is revealed, other than what we knew already. The television reporters and crews rush off to get it on the air at noon. I head back to the Prestwould to blog about it. The guy from the entertainment magazine is already posting his with his iPhone. You need one of those, Wheelie told me last week. Buy me one, I said.

The paper's as close as my apartment, but I still have fond hopes of sneaking in another hour or two of sleep after I feed the blogees.

Custalow is there. I'd forgotten he was taking the morning off. He had to attend to a plumbing emergency that ate up half his Saturday. Custalow isn't afraid of hard work, but he seems to have decided that he won't go the extra yard for the folks who were ready to fire him for theft last year.

He's watching one of the local channels. They've broken into some stupid-ass, bare-your-soul-in-front-of-strangers talk show with the breathless news that, yes, Richard Slade is arrested. It's safe to go outside again.

"You need somebody to dress you," Custalow says. I stand next to him and see myself on the screen, in the background. Maybe the jeans and the I AM THE MAN FROM NANTUCKET sweatshirt with chili stains on it weren't a great choice. Maybe I should have worn socks. And shaved. Maybe I should have gone home from Penny Lane two hours earlier last night.

"You might as well have worn your pajamas," he says, suppressing a laugh.

I suggest to Custalow that he could have saved me. He saw me headed out the door.

"I thought you must be going out for a walk, somewhere where nobody would see you."

Yeah, he's right. And I really don't want a male housemate asking, "Are you going to wear that?"

Custalow turns away from the TV as they switch back to a couple who seem to be having a very public discussion about his having sex with her sister, in their bed.

"I can't believe it," Custalow says, and I assume he's talking about Richard Slade, not the disaffected couple.

"What's so hard to believe? Who had a better motive?"

"It doesn't make any sense."

I sit back. Custalow chews his words for a while before he spits them out. You have to wait for it.

"He was in my cellblock for a while. I remember, at lunch one day, he got to talking. He didn't talk that much, so when he did, you listened."

Another pause.

"He said that if he did get out, all he was going to do was sit under the big shade tree in his momma's backyard, drink lemonade and watch the world go by. When it got cold, he said, he'd feed the birds, then sit in his momma's kitchen and watch them."

Pause.

"One of the young bucks on our block kind of laughs and asks him, 'How about the white bitch that put your ass in here. Ain't you got sumpin' for her?' By this time, most of us believed Slade when he said he didn't do it.

"Slade just looked at him for a minute. Then he said, 'That woman didn't know what she was doing. She didn't mean any harm.' And then he just got his tray and walked off."

"You don't think he killed her?"

"Anything's possible," Custalow said. "But if I gambled, I'd bet against it."

I blog, and then I nap. When I wake up, Custalow's gone to work. After I shower, shave and exchange the sweatshirt for a button-down, a sweater and a sports jacket, I do the same. I wouldn't have showered and shaved for the desk monkeys at the paper, especially on a day I'm not getting paid for, but I have another stop in mind.

At the office, somebody has already done a screen grab and has left a printout on my desk. There's the press conference, with the TV "talent" in their camel-hair overcoats, and there's me. Somebody got a red pen and drew a line to one of the talking heads standing next to me, then wrote in "TV journalist," then drew another line to me. That one was titled, "real journalist," but somebody had marked through it and wrote "homeless person asking TV journalist for spare change."

"Nice of you to dress," Sally Velez says.

"It's my day off. You're lucky I'm wearing pants."

"Very lucky."

I lean closer to her, so no one else can hear.

"That's not what you used to say."

Sally comes as close to blushing as she ever does.

"Are you writing the story?"

"No, I just went to the press conference to wipe Baer's butt."

She looks surprised.

"Baer was there?"

Mal Wheelwright is in his office.

"Wheelie," Sally calls over, "did you send Baer over to cover the chief's press conference?"

Wheelie, looking up and seeing me, looks embarrassed.

"Uh . . . yeah. He told me he'd cover it, since it was Willie's day off."

Every year at the state press contest awards dinner, where everybody's a winner, Mark Baer leads the league in shared awards. A good story turns up on somebody else's beat, and suddenly, there's Baer, "helping" and earning a byline or two for a sidebar, or stepping in when the reporter's been chasing the story for nine days and needs a break.

It only takes me a few minutes to bang out fifteen inches for the Tuesday paper. I tell Sally that there might be a write-through later.

She's already given my story a cursory read as I'm putting on my jacket.

"Where to now, Clark Kent?" she asks. "It's too early for happy hour."

"Always happy hour somewhere," I tell her. I blow her a kiss, and she graces me with the smallest of smiles and gives me the finger.

Philomena Slade's home is pretty easy to find. By the time I get there, the TV types have already gone. This isn't Los Angeles, and paparazzi might as well be some appetizer at Mamma Zu's.

Still, I don't relish this. I only hope a couple of large male relatives haven't been left in charge of dispatching snooping reporters. It's hard to hurt my feelings, but I have a strong aversion to pain.

I knock three times, then wait a few seconds and knock again.

Finally, the door opens. There's a storm door, locked, I'm sure, between me and Richard Slade's mother. I can barely see her with the sun reflecting off the glass.

"Go away," she says. I don't think she even realizes yet that I'm the SOB from the paper that she threw out of Marcus Green's Yukon a week ago.

"Please, Mrs. Slade," I say, trying to make myself heard through the storm door. "I'm not here to make trouble. I want to get his side of the story."

This goes about as far as I thought it would. She's starting to shut the door when I play the only card I have.

"Wait. Please. I'm Artie Lee's son."

The door shuts. I wait for about two seconds. The door opens.

She looks me up and down.

"Bull," she says.

Then, she opens the storm door and squints at me, giving me the once-over.

"You're passin'," she says.

As in passing for white. We both know it isn't necessary to "pass" these days. They get extra PC points where I work if they can claim you're black. But, yeah, maybe I have been passing, for about half a century.

She asks me who's my momma, and I give her a concise enough description of Peggy Black that she finally believes me.

"Peggy still smoking that weed?" she asks.

I tell her I think she's trying to quit. Yeah. She's down to a joint a day.

As I start to step inside, though, she stops me again.

"You're the one I had them throw out of Marcus Green's car. That reporter from the paper."

I wait, not bothering to deny it. Finally, though, family wins out.

"Well," she says, "come on in anyhow."

We go through a living room full of photographs and time-worn furniture, with a pre-flat-screen TV sitting in the corner. We dodge kids' toys, which seems strange until we get to the kitchen, where two little boys, maybe four years old, are sitting at the table, coloring.

"Momma Phil," one of them says, "look."

She offers the first smile of the day.

"That's very good, Jamal. Very good. You stayed between the lines and all, just like I told you to. Let's see, Jeroy. Umm. Yes. That's nice. Now, you all go on back to the bedroom. This gentleman and me have got to talk."

They ask her if they can watch TV, and she says maybe after a while. They whine a little but don't question her.

"That TV," she says, shaking her head.

I observe that she seems to have a way with kids.

She looks at me and kind of snorts.

"You caught 'em on a good day."

She says Jamal and Jeroy are her great-nephews, her niece's twins. She's keeping them while their mother works at the post office.

"You're related to them, I suppose. Chanelle would've been Artie's cousin, too. Anyhow, there's always somebody needs some help. And now I'm retired, I've got the time."

She offers me a Coke or some water. I can see when she opens the fridge that there's no beer.

"I'd meant to work until next year, when I'm sixty-five," she says, "but when I found out Richard was getting out . . ."

She pauses for a few seconds. She has her back to me, pouring the Coke. I see her left hand clench into a fist, then relax.

"It just seemed like a good time to quit."

She says she was a secretary for thirty-two years at Philip Morris, "long enough to pay for this place."

After an appropriate amount of time, I get around to asking what I came to ask. At first, it looks like she's just going to tell me to leave.

"Richard was here Friday night," she says at last. "Some folks came over, but they were gone by ten, and Richard went to bed right after that. He's used to going to bed early. He says he has trouble sleeping here, because it's so quiet."

Philomena says she went to bed right after the eleven o'clock news, and that Richard was asleep when she looked in on him at eleven thirty—in the bedroom she'd kept waiting for him to return to for the past twenty-eight years.

"Then, when I got up Saturday morning to fix breakfast, about seven, he was in here, watching that sports channel on the TV. You could tell that he'd just woke up.

"I told the police that, told 'em three times, but they believe what they want to believe."

She's chopping up some onions, getting supper ready for the boys, or maybe just for herself. She turns toward me and points with her hand, still holding an impressive chopping knife.

"He didn't do it. He didn't do it twenty-eight years ago, and he didn't do it now."

I'm not inclined to argue with anybody holding a knife that big, but I wonder. Is it possible that Richard Slade could have left the house, done the deed and come back before his mother got up? The shooting happened about a quarter past five. He would have had time.

I ask her about her car. There's a ten-year-old Camry outside on the street, which must be hers.

"I keep the keys in my purse," she says. "I keep my purse by my bedside table. I told the police that, too."

Well, he could have jump-started it. Or, he could have just gotten somebody else to do the deed. Slade probably knew a character or two, from nearly three decades as a guest of the state, who could have done it for him. Or maybe it was just a cousin or a nephew. Maybe revenge takes a village, too.

Philomena shows me his room. There are trophies, from Little League baseball and pee-wee football, then a few from junior high and high school. She probably dusted them off every week, waiting.

"He was quite an athlete," she says, "and he was full of himself, the way boys are. He was running with some boys that he shouldn't of been running with. And I was always on him about his grades. But he was a good boy.

"He always told me not to worry, that he was going to go to college and make me proud."

When they heard the news, later on Saturday, about Alicia Simpson's murder, Philomena says Richard just "kind of wilted."

"'Oh, lord, Momma,' he told me. 'They gonna think I did it.'"

She says it was all she could do to keep him from running, right then.

"I told him, 'You stay right here, and when they come asking questions, you and I both know where you were, and we'll tell 'em.'

"And we did, like it did any good. They came for him on Sunday morning, just as we were getting ready to go to church. They took him away, and they stayed here and asked me the same damn—excuse me—the same questions over and over. And telling them the truth didn't seem to matter."

I ask her if she thinks Richard would like to talk to somebody from the newspaper, to give his side of the story.

"I don't know. I'd have to ask Marcus Green."

Well, I should have figured that one out. I can't believe our premier bomb-throwing mouthpiece hasn't already called a press conference of his own.

I tell her I'll call Mr. Green myself.

At the door, she puts her hand around my wrist. She's strong for such a wiry woman.

"You come back, now," she says. "You're family, even if you do work for that newspaper."

CHAPTER SEVEN

Tuesday

I'm fifteen minutes late. Caught unawares, before she can give me hell for making her wait, Kate is adorable. She's seated facing the wall, with the left side of her face visible to me. She does that thing where she grips her lower lip with her teeth while she does something deathly important on the iPhone. A strand of her brownish-red hair hangs loose. She has started wearing reading glasses. Maybe she's been wearing them awhile. Paying attention wasn't one of my strong suits. She's frowning a little. I used to put my hands on her forehead when she did that and smooth the frown lines out. Usually, I was the one who had put them there.

She doesn't see me until I reach down and tuck the stray strand behind her ear. She jerks her head around and sees that it's me, and the look turns from one of surprise to the kind you give a delinquent child who has met your expectations.

"I figured I'd better get here on time," she says. "If I waited for you, they might have given our table away."

Well, no. Not likely. Looking around Can Can, with its loose approximation of a Paris bistro, I see plenty of empty tables. In the Great Recession, some seem to have forgone *moules frites*.

Still, point taken. Yes, it is a sign of disrespect to always be the waitee instead of the waiter. But I've already been around to Marcus Green's office and been told he's in court and will be in about two. And then I stopped by Penny Lane for a quick pint, and then a photographer I used to work with before he got laid off dropped in, and we talked for another pint. Time slips away.

She puts away the iPhone.

"This Richard Slade case," she says, never one for useless verbs. "Any sense in even having the trial before the hanging?"

Kate likes to play devil's advocate. If you say the sun comes up in the east, she wants to discuss alternative possibilities.

"I am not," she told me once, when we were arguing about global warming, "a yes woman."

I tell her that they don't really do hangings in Virginia anymore, even for black men who kill white women; but the odds seem to favor either a very long stay in a very bad place or an eventual enforced overdose of some very lethal chemicals.

"But he seems so, I don't know, so innocent."

"You got that from watching on TV? They didn't even get to tape him doing the perp walk."

"I met him."

"Where? When?"

She gives me a sly smile. As was often the case in our shared past, Kate's ahead of me.

"Yesterday at the jail. I went with Marcus Green."

Kate knew Marcus back in the day. I can't remember now if I introduced him to her or if she knew him first. He'd been a good source, a quote machine, as long as you knew that he had his own agenda and it might not jibe with yours. I haven't talked to him much since I went back on night cops, but he doesn't seem to have changed much.

At any rate, we've all had a few drinks together over the years.

The Green connection probably explains then why Kate asked me to meet her for lunch today. Her calls to me usually are along the lines of "Why haven't I gotten the rent check yet?" When she moved out, we reached an agreement. She pays the mortgage and I pay the rent. My ex-wife is my landlady.

"He said he was impressed with what I did in the Martin Fell case."

I note that there wasn't really any "case," since the common-wealth's attorney chose to free Mr. Fell long before it ever came to trial, mostly due to the efforts of yours truly.

"Still," she says, "he liked how I took a chance. He said he liked anybody with balls enough to sass Bartley, Bowman and Bush and get away with it."

"So," I say, wishing I could smoke indoors, "you're going to work with Marcus Green? I guess that had something to do with my lunch invitation."

She graces me with a ten-watt smile.

"Could be. I just wanted to talk, about Richard Slade and all. You know all the history."

I fill her in. For some reason, I don't tell her about my recent visit with Philomena Slade, but I do tell her Abe Custalow's assessment.

"Well, Abe's pretty astute," Kate says. 'Astute' isn't a word I usually associate with my old friend, ex-con and housemate, but it's probably pretty apt.

She frowns. I resist the urge.

"The guy seems real," she says, and I deduce that she's talking about Slade. "I mean, there's nothing about him that indicates he might have killed somebody for revenge. He just seemed, I don't know, befuddled, like he couldn't figure it all out."

Kate's munching on the "quiche de la semaine." I ordered a cheeseburger with French fries, "although I guess you just call them 'fries' in here." The waiter didn't get the joke. Kate winced.

I tell her that I'm not willing to write Richard Slade out of the book of life just yet, either, even if the police think they've got this one tied up with a nice little bow on top.

"Maybe he got somebody else to do it for him," I say as Kate directs me to wipe ketchup off my chin. "He could've orchestrated the whole thing and had it done while he was sleeping at his momma's."

"Anyhow," she says. "I thought maybe we could work together, share information and all that."

"That could work," I tell her. It did last time. She got a gold star from BB&B. I got one of those three-dollar Virginia Press Association awards. Wheelie even nominated me for a Pulitzer, which is not so impressive when you realize that you can nominate the weekly school lunch menu listing for a Pulitzer, as long as the check doesn't bounce.

"There's something else," I tell her, after we've chitchatted a bit and she's insisted on picking up the tab.

She looks up from figuring out the tip.

"What?"

"I think the defendant is my second cousin."

I explain my convoluted kinship with Richard Slade, mentioning Philomena without telling Kate I've seen her in the last twenty-four hours.

"Well," she says, "you might ought to recuse yourself from the case."

I remind her that I'm a newspaperman, not a lawyer. Plus, nobody at the paper knows, yet, that Slade and I share a couple of great-grandparents.

"So," she says, "can we, you know, meet once in a while, compare notes and such?"

I nod. Why not?

We walk out together, but we're parked in different directions.

I ask her how things are going with Mr. Ellis, her present husband.

"His name's Greg. Everything's fine. But thanks for asking. Headed in to work?"

I tell her I'm on my way to see Marcus Green.

Green's office is on Franklin Street, close enough to the paper that I can use the company parking deck and walk there.

He is a lone wolf, no partners, just a couple of assistants, one of whom tells me that she will check and see if Mr. Green is in.

Soon, the door to his office opens and he comes bursting out like the place is on fire.

"Willie! How's my favorite muckraker? Come on in!"

He slaps my back and gives me a man-hug.

Even if Marcus Green was going to shoot you, he'd treat you like you were his long lost brother. Even if you wanted to shoot him, he'd probably be able to jolly you out of it, if he was trying. The night-and-day aspect of his personality works well in the courtroom and elsewhere. He can make you want to be his best friend and, in the blink of an eye, cop that menacing, fuck-with-me attitude he uses on witnesses and others he wishes to bend to his will.

"Still got your penthouse apartment?"

I tell him that Kate is still my landlady.

He laughs. He has the kind of booming laugh that makes people want to tell him their funniest joke.

"I don't think I'd like giving either one of my exes the option of kicking me to the curb. Although I do write them each a check every month." He laughs again, then turns down the volume, goes all solemn on me.

"So, what's this about?"

I tell him, like he doesn't know already.

"Do you think there's a chance I might be able to talk with your client? His mother said I'd need to check with you."

"You got Philomena to talk to you? Damn, Willie. You are a helluva reporter."

I don't tell him, just yet, about my trump card.

"Thanks, by the way, for letting her put my ass out in the middle of the East End the other day."

Green shrugs.

"It was her call. She was somewhat upset with that racist rag you work for. I don't blame her, actually."

I wonder to myself what our editorial department has cooked up in the aftermath of Richard Slade's arrest. I'm surprised there wasn't something in this morning's paper.

I ask him again about meeting with Slade.

He frowns and says he'll consider it.

"Well," I tell him, "you might as well have the whole family working with you. Me, you and Kate. The Mod Squad."

"Ah. So you know about that. Well, I know she's on the side of the angels. I'm not so sure about you. You're more like the guy with an angel on one shoulder and a devil on the other one, both whispering in your ears."

There doesn't seem to be any way around it.

"My father and Philomena were first cousins."

He absorbs this, never showing any sign of surprise. I would hate to play poker with Marcus Green. Actually, the thought of him at one of our Oregon Hill sessions with Custalow, McGonnigal, Andy Peroni and the rest is amusing.

"I always thought you were one of us," Green says. "Something about the way you carry yourself, your hair, something."

I doubt it, but if I can win the hand with this particular hole card, so be it.

"Let me see if my client is amenable to your request."

I look him in the eye.

"He'll be amenable if you tell him to be."

Marcus Green gives me a look that could cut diamonds. Then he nods.

"Could be," he says. "Could be. We'll have to pray over that one."

I put up with this bullshit because, for all his grandstanding and playacting, he has walked the walk, a burr in the power structure's ass since he got out of law school. No name causes more consternation at the Commonwealth Club, where the white-haired great-grandsons of the Confederacy have their bourbon and water with a shot of bile.

He walks me to the door, then stops. He pins me with the look he usually saves for his final summations. His face is like a fist, hard and ready.

"Know this. Richard Slade did not kill that woman, no matter how much some people want it to be so."

I nod. He dials The Look back a notch.

"Please give my regards to Kate," he says, and I remind him that he's likely to see her before I do.

The most mellifluous laugh in Richmond follows me out into the street.

I have time for a Camel between Marcus Green's office and the paper. I'm a block away when my cellphone rings.

"Willie," Sarah Goodnight says, "they're at it again."

My ID badge still works, although the guard at the front desk looks a little more alert, or at least awake, than usual.

As soon as I come out of the elevator, the tension hits me like a blast of sewer air. Rumors have been perching on our computer terminals like buzzards for weeks. Advertising is down. Circulation is down. Expenses aren't down far enough. Today, it appears, is the day.

There's a clot of people over by the features department, where some decidedly uncomfortable-looking human resources boy is watching Beth Reynolds clean out her desk. Jesus Christ, Beth Reynolds has been here longer than I have, and she does what nobody else in the newsroom wants to do. She deals with the brides and—God help her—the brides' mothers. When they come parading in, determined that absolutely nothing is going to screw up the social event of their lives, that they are not going to brook any sass from some newspaper flunky, Beth is on the receiving end, defusing them and at the same time preserving whatever dignity our poor tree-killing anachronism clings to. When we get the brides' photos and IDs somehow mixed up, Beth is the one who catches the mistake and averts disaster. Three years ago, we managed to switch photos of a truck driver who'd just saved a woman's life in a car fire with that of a very self-important bride. Before she was done, Beth had appeased not only the trucker but both the bride and her mother. If we sent Beth Reynolds to Washington, she could make the Republicans lie down with the Democrats.

And now, apparently, she's gone. Another one bites the dust.

"There's six that we know of," Sally Velez says before she goes over to offer condolences to a fifty-seven-year-old woman who's about to not have health insurance.

A photographer, a page designer, a copy editor, a sportswriter, Beth Reynolds and an assistant city editor. Chip, chip, chip.

"By the way," Sally adds, "Wheelie wants to see you. He and Grubby."

She sees me blanch.

"Don't worry," she says. "They're not going to fire your ass. Not now, anyhow."

"How do you know?" I figure I must be near the top of the managing editor's and publisher's shit lists.

"All the ones that have been axed so far, they got calls from upstairs this morning."

I check my voice mail back at the apartment, then start breathing again. This place makes me crazy, but what else am I going to do? Media relations?

I walk past Enos Jackson, who looks a little pale. He's already been brought back from the dead once, thanks to a little secret agreement between me and Grubby, and he doesn't know that he is—unless Grubby himself gets hauled away—more or less golden.

"You're next," I tell him. He doesn't seem to think it's funny.

Up on the fourth floor, Sandy McCool looks a little flustered, at least compared with her usual unflappable self. When Pete Bocelli in sports did a face-down in the lunchroom two years ago, it was Sandy who had the defibrillator out and working its magic in about thirty seconds while everybody else was crapping their pants. She saved his fat-ass life, then went back and finished her sandwich.

But Sandy's the one, I know, who always has to make The Call, the one who then has to see a lifetime of friends and acquaintances come trudging up and then trudging out, escorted by HR, some of them in tears, some of them glaring at her as if she were responsible.

"Tough day," I say. Sandy gives me a nod so small and tight that the security camera might not have caught it. Sandy's divorced with two kids in college.

Wheelie comes puffing in, shaking his head and muttering something about how much he hates all this. He straightens his tie as we walk past Sandy and into the *sanctum sanctorum*.

James H. Grubbs doesn't bother to stand up. He motions for us to take a seat. He looks a little haggard, pale even by Grubby's standards. It really can't be that much fun to fire people who once befriended you as a young reporter. But Grubby's got the MBA playbook, the one that says the only morality is what's good for the company. Coincidentally, doing what's good for the company is good for Grubby, who can always take a Xanax when he needs a good night's sleep.

"I wanted to get an update on what's going on with the Simpson murder."

Wheelie fills him in.

"So, we're done with this one, until the trial?"

Wheelie nods his head.

I clear my throat. I should shut up. I can't.

"Not exactly."

Grubby acts as if he was expecting it. I hear Wheelie groan.

"Not exactly?"

I tell them both about my conversations with Philomena Slade and Marcus Green.

"His mother and his lawyer don't think he did it?" Grubby says. "Well, we'd better get all over that, then. Stop the presses."

"I'm not saying he didn't do it. But I think we ought to look around a little, see if things check out."

"Well, I don't think so. So don't do it."

I'm a little surprised, I must say. Grubby is a cautious man, but he isn't above selling newspapers, and he's got to know that this story has everything the circulation department could ever hope for.

He looks at Wheelie.

"We're done here," he says, and my managing editor gets up to go.

I start to say something else, but Wheelie takes me by the arm. I shut up and leave.

"What the fuck?" I inquire back downstairs in Wheelie's office. "We're dropping this?"

"No," Wheelie says. "We're just not going to create our own news. The arraignment's tomorrow, right? After that, we'll wait for the trial."

"What is this all about?"

Wheelie shuts the door.

"Just between you and me," he says. "This never, ever leaves this room."

I nod.

"It's about the Whitehursts."

The penny drops. The Whitehursts own the paper, have owned the paper since before the Civil War. Grubby is the first non-family publisher, and everybody in Richmond knows his predecessor isn't just sitting back and giving the new boy free rein. Giles Whitehurst, a hale and blustery eight-five with no heirs desiring a career in newspapering, is still the chairman of the board, and chairman of the board trumps publisher.

"Did you know," Wheelie asks, "that Giles Whitehurst and Harper Simpson were fraternity brothers at U.Va.?"

I confess that I am deficient in my knowledge of Alicia Simpson's father.

"Well, apparently, the sister went to Daddy, who called Grubby and told him to back off, that the family has been through enough anguish already. They just want it dropped."

I wonder out loud why Lewis Simpson Witt would think we weren't dropping it.

"Maybe she knows something about the way you stick that big nose of yours into everybody's business."

"You know what they say, Wheelie. Big nose, big . . ."

"Yeah, yeah. Just let this one ride, though. I don't want Sandy giving you a wakeup call."

He grimaces as he looks out into the newsroom, where a photographer is being gently led out of the building carrying a cardboard box. He looks our way and pauses long enough to balance the box on his hip with one hand and give Wheelie the finger.

"Don't worry," I tell Mal Wheelwright, "anything I do, I do on my own. They won't be able to trace it back to you."

Wheelie groans again. It is not the response he was hoping for. I can't help that. Now I'm interested. All of my best stories have come after somebody told me to back off. Most of my worst screw-ups have, too.

As I put my hand on the door handle, Wheelie says, "Wait."

I wait.

"You're off the story."

I wait some more.

"There isn't anything more to write anyhow, Willie. We're just going to have Baer pick it up. He'll cover the arraignment."

"This is nuts. Baer doesn't know shit about this case."

"He's a quick learner."

"Goddammit, Wheelie, you're giving this story away. There's more to this. Go back up there and tell that son of a bitch we're a newspaper. Grow a pair, for God's sake."

Even as I say it, I know my mouth has again outrun my brain.

Wheelie turns kind of pale, and then his face starts to glow. He comes around his desk so fast that at first I think he's going to hit me, and my last act here will be to punch out the managing editor.

"Don't you ever talk to me like that again, even in here with the door closed," he says. "I argued your case before you ever got there. I lost, OK? Unlike some people, when I'm overruled, I do what's best for the team. Unlike some people, who shall remain you, I'm a team player."

I have several other things on the tip of my tongue. They're waiting in line, actually, dying for their moment on the stage.

But, for once, my brain reels them all back in before they can slip past my teeth. I apologize and slip out quietly. Right now, I don't need to be headed out the door carrying a cardboard box.

CHAPTER EIGHT

Wednesday

This morning, the only mention of the Alicia Parker Simpson murder is in editorial.

Apparently, Giles Whitehurst, Lewis Witt and the rest of the Simpson family are not opposed to certain kinds of publicity. Our crack editorial writers, defenders of truth, justice and the white American way, took Richard Slade to the woodshed. They even saw his arrest as a repudiation of DNA testing, somehow. (Editorially, we're not big fans of science around here. See: evolution, global warming.)

Some of our readers will smack their lips over their Cheerios and nod approvingly, shaking their heads over fuzzy-headed criminal coddlers who would turn such a man as this loose again. Many others, no doubt, will believe that we are once again afflicting the afflicted. Maybe that's why we don't have as many readers as we once did. But that's just my opinion.

I'm hanging out the window over Monroe Park, trying to direct Camel smoke in that direction, when the phone rings. Custalow gets it. Holding the phone in his hand, he mouths "Kate."

I remind her, before she can get really wound up, that I don't write the editorials.

"I know that," she says. "But how can you work for those people?"

I tell her I'll quit tomorrow if she'll stop charging me rent.

"I just might," she says. We're both bluffing.

She asks me if I'm going to the arraignment. I tell her I'm off the story.

"But I still plan to be there," I add. I don't think Wheelie and Grubby will fire me for that. I think I'm free to do what I want when they're not paying me.

"So, I guess you're not going to be much help to us."

"Does that mean you're definitely on the defense team?"

"If, by 'team,' you mean Marcus and me, yes."

I tell her that I'm still not sure about Richard Slade, but that I want to check around a little more.

"On your own time?"

"If that's what it takes. But I'm not going to get my ass fired over this."

She snorts.

"Getting fired from that place would be like getting evicted from the bus station bathroom."

I tell her I'll see her at the arraignment.

It's going to be a busy day. In addition to the arraignment, services for Alicia Simpson are scheduled for three P.M. I told Sally Velez that I'd be in by five-ish (without, of course, giving the funeral as the reason). Since I have one less story to cover than I did a day ago, I have some time on my hands.

When I get to the courtroom, I see a sparse crowd consisting mostly of news media types. Philomena Slade is sitting by herself a couple of rows back. The entourage that was there to celebrate her son's freedom has vanished. It is as invisible as it apparently was for the twenty-eight years he was locked up.

"Mind if I sit here?" I ask her.

She seems to take a couple of seconds to recognize me. Then she tells me to get the hell away from her. She obviously has read our paper, including the editorial pages. All things considered, I can't believe she subscribes. I move two rows back. In the same row on the other side, Mark Baer looks surprised to see me. I ignore him, and the judge comes in before Baer can ask me what the hell I'm doing here.

Richard Slade is bedecked in an orange jumpsuit and hand-cuffs. It doesn't take long for him to be charged with first-degree murder. It doesn't even take that long for the judge to deny bail. Marcus Green's face is a billboard, telling the world what a gross injustice has been done to his client, but it's all for show. Everybody in Richmond knew how this was going to turn out.

They take him away, and we all leave. On the steps outside, Green gives our assembled fact-gatherers a lecture on the right of every man to have his day in court and not be tried in the news media. He looks meaningfully at me when he says that.

"Before this lamentable episode is over," he says, actually shaking his fist, "some of those who have appointed themselves as this innocent man's judges will hide their faces in shame."

Well, I doubt it, but it's a nice thought, if Marcus is right.

Out of the corner of my eye, I see Philomena walking toward her beat-up Camry. She looks as defeated as I've seen her. I decide to try again. All the others are still in the thrall of Marcus Green.

I reach her before she can get in her car and lock the doors.

"Ms. Slade. Philomena. Wait."

She tries to get around me. I move with her in an awkward dance to keep her from getting into the car until I can convince her, again, that I am not the devil.

"Get away from me," she says, and I can see that she is near tears.

"I'm on his side," I tell her. "I want to find out what happened."

"You already know what happened. I told you what happened. And then you all went and wrote that, that stuff. Family, my behind."

"It wasn't me. They don't ask my opinion on editorials."

She finally manages to get past me and into her car. Before she slams the door, she looks up at me.

"I think we both know which side you're on. You're gettin' a nice salary, it looks like to me."

As she starts the car and speeds away, all defenses of my righteousness and purity in this sorry episode curdle in my mouth like sour milk.

Baer finally catches up with me as Philomena is leaving.

"What are you doing here?" he asks. He seems a little winded. I can see already the pudgy middle-aged hack he's morphing into. It's always sad when you see them come here fresh out of college, all lean and hungry, and then you watch them put on a couple or three pounds a year and start losing their youth a day at a time. Although, with Baer, it's not all that sad. He is an opportunist, and I don't really like opportunists.

I tell him that I'm exercising my right as a citizen, that I wanted to get a close look at how our judicial system works.

"You know that I'm covering it, though, right?"

"That's what they tell me."

"They just thought maybe you were, like, too close to the case."

Too close as in asking too many questions. But neither Grubby not the Simpson family, and certainly not Mark Baer, knows just how close to this case I am, at least not yet.

"So who was that?" he nods in the direction of Philomena Slade's now departed car.

He probably ought to know her on sight, but I tell him.

"His mother? You talked to his mother?"

"Tried to. After that editorial this morning, she wasn't in the mood."

"Yeah," Baer says, agreeing with me for once. "That was a little hard to swallow."

I turn to leave. Baer stops me.

"But, you don't have any reason to believe he didn't do it?"

I tell him I don't know anything. Yet.

"But you're going to find out. I know you."

"I'm not empowered to find out. I'm off the story, remember?"

He doesn't believe a word of it, but he lets me go.

Marcus Green has finished dispensing quotes, and he and Kate are waiting for me.

"Those guys," Marcus says, shaking his head. "They eat this stuff up. Oh, wait. Did I say that out loud?"

He gives me a quick grin, then looks around to make sure no TV camera is there to catch him not looking like Frederick Douglass with a hangover.

"But seriously," Kate says, "how can they just write something like that without waiting for any kind of trial, without any kind of hard facts at all?"

"Well, they did preface it with, 'If the facts are as they appear to be.'"

"Yeah, that was considerate. And then they went on for ten paragraphs excoriating our client as the lowest form of scum." She reminded me that, last year, the paper urged the "utmost caution in rushing to judgment" when one of our leading state senators was arrested for shooting his wife to death. Then, after his slam-dunk conviction, they expressed their sorrow over "the downfall of a man who has done the Commonwealth much good."

"They might be doing us a favor," Marcus says. "Maybe they can editorialize us into a change of venue."

I note that his client might have a better chance keeping his business in the city and not depending on some suburban or deep country jury for his deliverance.

I ask them if they want to join me at Perly's for either late breakfast or early lunch. Marcus Green has to get back to his office. Kate, who usually turns down such offers from me, surprises me by saying yes. Breaking bread with her twice in two days will set the post-marital record.

"I'm on a kind of leave of absence," she tells me when we're seated and I remark on her willingness to blow off an hour or so of company time. It turns out that Bartley, Bowman and Bush isn't all that thrilled about Kate working on this particular case. When I think about it, it makes sense. The old partners in her firm have, like Giles Whitehurst, probably had more than a few bourbons with Harper Simpson and would like to distance themselves from his daughter's alleged murderer.

Kate confirms this when she tells me that old Felix Bowman was one of the founding members of the Quarry.

"Blood's pretty thick around here," I observe.

She can use BB&B's offices for now, and she can come back to the land of the living when she's finished with this case, presumably with no ill effects. Or so they say.

There's something else, though. Kate would deny it, but I was not consistently and completely oblivious to her when we were married. I knew when she was holding back, when she had a bug up her butt.

We finally get around to it, about the time she's finishing the last of her eggs.

"I guess you could say I'm kind of on leave from Greg, too."

There aren't many things an ex-husband can say about that without stepping on a tender part of his anatomy. So I shut up and let her talk, pitching in with the occasional "I see" and "uh-huh" to keep things flowing.

There's nothing original or startling in what she's telling me. Mr. and Mrs. Ellis have decided on a little unofficial trial separation "just to figure out where we're headed." They don't seem to have as much in common as they once thought they did. I think but don't say that this is often the case.

"I don't know why I'm telling you all this," she says.

"Maybe because I can keep a secret?"

She shakes her head.

"No. Hell, everybody's going to know about it anyway."

Kate isn't completely unlike me, God help her. Maybe there are some people who just aren't meant to say the magic words and spend the rest of their lives never considering all the roads not taken.

"Well," I say, looking at my watch, "I'd better go home and change."

"You're going to the funeral?"

"Yeah, I thought I would."

"Would you mind if I came back to the Prestwould with you? I could wait while you change. I'm about as dressed for a funeral as I intend to be. We could go together."

She graces me with a smile that hints of very un-Kate-like shyness.

"I'd like to see what you've done with—or to—the place."

Probably not the best idea, but we've each had a Bloody Mary, and I can't think of a reason to say no, other than "What will the neighbors think?" Which would be a very stupid thing to say right now. It would indicate that I believe my ex has something in mind other than convenience and a chance to see the inside of the place for which she pays the mortgage.

So she follows me over and parks in a visitor's spot.

McGrumpy is, as always, ensconced in the lobby. He makes a point of having a very courtly conversation with Kate, who never seemed to mind him as much as I do. She tells him that we're going to Alicia Simpson's funeral service. So is McGrumpy, along with about half the Prestwould. At least three of our residents are near or distant cousins. There are about a million and a quarter people living in the general vicinity, but then there's the small village, undetectable to the untrained eye, of Old Richmond, carrying seven generations of history to the latest wedding or funeral.

"Well," McGrumpy says, lifting his ancient eyebrows in an approximation of juvenile salaciousness that makes me want to smack him, "you all have a nice visit."

There is every probability that there will be some mention of Kate's impromptu visit in the next *Prestwould Post*, whose gossip column is co-written by McGrumpy. Jesus.

Upstairs, I am happy to see that Custalow is absent, working on some balky part of our ancient building.

Kate sniffs the air as we walk down the thirty-foot hallway leading to the living room, but she doesn't mention anything about illicit smoking. I've been pretty careful. The hallway was what hooked her on the place, I think, made her feel like we had to have it. The walls are what I called pink and she called coral, with a couple of pillars halfway down. I'd never tell Kate this, but it reeked of the old-money Richmond her middle-class heart must have secretly coveted while she was overworking her way to summa cum laude and through law school.

"Not bad," she says, obviously pleased not to see empty pizza boxes on the coffee table or a week of dirty dishes in the sink. "Abe must be keeping you straight."

"I've had some practice at not being a slob."

"Yeah," she says, smirking. "I remember."

"It wasn't that bad. I always had clean underwear."

She looks up at me and feeds me my lines.

"Do you still?"

There might as well be a teleprompter in front of me.

"Why," I ask, regretting my words while I say them, "don't we go and find out?"

CHAPTER NINE

The services at St. Paul's are over by two forty-five. We gave Clara a ride, and she is among the chosen few dozen who have been invited to Lewis and Carl Witt's afterward. I'm not so sure that the Witts included us in that inner circle, but, hey, I'm driving.

The crowd at the downtown church was, as I'd expected, out the door. Despite the fact that Alicia Simpson had been seen as almost a recluse by the outside world, she had a lot of friends— from St. Catherine's and Sweet Briar and, according to the obituary, various boards and committees. And then, there were the gawkers, people who might have known the family and had nothing better to do on a Wednesday afternoon than put on a suit and go see how the rich handle tragedy. We used to have an obit writer who called it funeral porn.

At the Witts, the crowd is somewhat more select, present company excepted. The old Tudor that Carl inherited from his father looks like it could have been, as was the case with a slightly larger concoction farther west, taken apart in Merry Olde England and reassembled on the banks of the James. Perhaps only in Richmond would this not look out of place.

In the receiving line, Lewis is polite enough to me. She probably thinks I'm using Clara Westbrook to pick the lock on her front door, but Clara helps me out there by introducing us and explaining that she needed a ride to the funeral, and was able to prevail on "these nice young friends" to accommodate.

"We've met," Lewis says, giving me a completely neutral smile. "I didn't know you were friends of Clara's." She says it in a way that indicates that this seems an unlikely match. Lewis probably can smell Oregon Hill on me.

Kate is smitten, as she often is among people with money. She says all the right things to Lewis and Carl. I am fortunate to have two charming women with me to smooth any rough spots my appearance might have produced.

Next to Carl is a man who appears to be about my age, although it's hard to tell. I shake hands with him and offer my condolences.

"Hi," he says, "I'm, ah, Wes," like he forgot his name for a half-second. He grips my hand like a drowning man reaching for salvation. I can feel a slight tremble in it before I pull away.

Alicia's brother looks like he'd rather be just about anywhere else.

He's a tall man, maybe six-three, with spiky, steel-gray hair. The frown crease above his nose, along with the bloodshot eyes with enough baggage under them for a trip to China, more or less negate the smile he attempts. He looks at me like a kid who doesn't know it's not polite to stare.

Kate is pleasant enough to him. Then, Clara, who has lingered to speak quietly with Lewis, comes up and gives him a full-blown Clara hug, complete with tears.

"I haven't seen you in so long," she says. He is looking over her shoulder, in my direction. He gives a kind of "what can you do?" shrug.

The Witts seem to have an entourage of servants, at least on this sad occasion, who come around with scallops wrapped in bacon, little tomato-cheese-and-parsley things on toast, Smithfield ham biscuits and other tidbits that seem more appropriate for a cocktail party than a day like this. Hell, maybe it's supposed to be a party. Celebration of life and all that crap. Hey, I want kegs and my favorite blues band at my going-away bash.

Nobody, though, seems much in a festive mood. Lives that end at forty-four don't elicit a whole lot of giddiness, in my experience. The Witts and their friends handle it better, or at least more sedately, than the East End families of drug war casualties, but dead is still dead.

I feel a tap on my shoulder and turn around to face a woman who looks to be about five feet tall, in her early forties, kind of cute, nice, well-preserved body, blonde this month.

"I need to talk to you," she says, and I say fine.

"Not here," she says, and demands my cellphone number. I'm inclined to give attractive women pretty much anything they want.

"I'll call you," she says, looking over her shoulder the way some of our editors at the paper do when they're bitching and worry that one of Grubby's snitches might be within earshot. Then she's gone.

Clara spends half an hour talking with old friends, and Kate finds a couple of lawyer acquaintances to chat with. Between ham biscuits, I call Sally and tell her I might be a tad late.

"Get here when you can," she says. "If you're gone two or three days, Wheelie might notice."

I see the mystery woman across the room and ask Clara who she is.

"Which one?" she says. "Oh, there. That's Bitsy. Susan Winston-Jones. She and Alicia are—were—close."

As we're leaving, Lewis puts her hand on Kate's arm.

"I understand," she says, "that you're defending my sister's murderer."

Says it as calm as dawn, as Peggy used to say. I don't know how she has learned that already, probably gleaned it from someone here at the death party. There's definitely a pipeline that moves the news faster than our printing presses do.

Kate is thrown for a couple of seconds, which seems to have been the intent.

"I am defending the man accused of that, yes," she says at last, and I'm proud of her for not doing the hummina-hummina, not apologizing or making excuses.

"Good day," is all Lewis Witt says before turning her back to us.

"That went well," I observe.

Clara seems perplexed. The possibility that Alicia Simpson's murder wasn't as cut-and-dried as our editorial pages say it was hasn't occurred to her.

"Well," she says, "I'm sure there's more than one side to the story."

Kate, who still can let herself be bothered by the knowledge that she has displeased one of the elite, in spite of all her efforts to do otherwise, gives Clara a hug.

"Do you think," Clara says, "that we could go by the Quarry?"

It's already four thirty. It'll be dark in less than an hour. It's cold as a witch's tit.

"Sure, why not?"

Kate shrugs and says she has nowhere particular to be.

Clara, it turns out, is on a committee in charge of making whatever minor repairs the place needs. A couple of jackleg carpenters are supposed to have fixed a small hole in the roof over the dressing rooms. A tree branch fell on it after the last storm.

"I just want to make sure it's covered," Clara says. "It's supposed to snow next week."

It's only five minutes away. Clara gives me the key, and I open the gate and drive us as close to the building as possible.

We all get out, and Clara steps back far enough to determine that there is, indeed, some kind of patch on the roof. She nods her head and says, "Good."

She looks out across the Quarry. What's left of the sun has lit it up so that it looks like a pit full of gold instead of water.

"We had some good times here," she says, leaning on her cane. She has risked leaving the oxygen bottle at home, and she's hoarding her breaths like she knows she doesn't have an infinite number of them left. "Alicia was such a good swimmer. I taught them how, you know. The two youngest ones anyway. Her and Wesley."

I ask her to fill me in on Wesley. All I've had so far is the shorthand version.

"Can we go sit in the car?" Clara asks. "I need to warm my rear end."

There are few joys, in my experience, equal to stepping from a windy, chilly January day into a heated car, with the late afternoon sun streaming in, and listening to a good story while the sun and the heater warm your bones. All that's missing is a pint of bourbon to pass around. Can't have everything.

Clara is a born storyteller, one who remembers the small details and hasn't picked up the annoying habit of telling the same tale two or three times.

"Wesley must be forty-six now, because he's two years older than Alicia," she says, shielding her eyes from the glare. I pull down the visor.

"He was a wonderful boy. Made straight A's and was on all the ball teams. Baseball, football, basketball. He could beat Harper at golf by the time he was thirteen, and Harper was good. Simone called him her golden boy."

But then, he came home from school one day and said he didn't think he could go back. He had started hearing voices, telling him to do things. Eventually, he would heed the voices when he didn't think he could do otherwise. A garage set on fire, a "borrowed" car wrecked, a neighbor's cat hanged.

"It was so awful," Clara says. "It seemed like one minute he was this All-American boy, mowing our lawn, looking you in the eye and talking to you like an adult, but polite, 'Yes, ma'am' and 'Yes, sir,' like he still knew he was a kid. He told them in the ninth grade that he was going to Princeton, Harper said."

"And then," Clara says, snapping her fingers "just like that, he changed."

They tried everything money could buy. The best shrinks, private schools that focused on "special" students, every kind of magic dust some drug company could come up with that might help but didn't.

"The worst thing," Clara says, "was that day at the Quarry."

She thinks it was about a year after Wesley was first diagnosed as schizophrenic. He was there with his parents and Alicia.

"I remember it was Fourth of July weekend, so the place was packed. Old Richmond all in one little knot there. I was sitting at one of the picnic tables, with the Tayloes, I think, when suddenly we heard this commotion.

"And then I hear Harper yell, 'Get back in there. Get back in there, goddammit.' Excuse me.

"We all look up, and there's Wesley, naked as a jaybird, walking and running toward the water, with Harper right behind him, trying to catch him. He runs out on the diving board and jumps in.

"He was a good swimmer. He must have stayed out there in the deep water for fifteen minutes at least, mooning everybody and giving us the finger. Harper just stood on the beach and finally gave up even trying to coax him in. By that time, I think Simone had gone to the car."

He finally had to come in, and by then whatever had gotten into him seemed to have gotten out again. Harper threw a towel around him, Clara said, and more or less dragged him to the car, with Alicia in tow.

"I heard a smack, we all did, and then Alicia screaming, 'Don't you hit him! Don't you hit Wesley!'"

Clara sighs.

"I never saw Wesley at the Quarry again. I don't know if he was banned or not, but after that, it was like he was invisible."

Finally, his father just seemed willing to cut his losses.

"Harper and Wesley had been close, closer than most fathers and sons, and I think what happened just killed something in Harper. He couldn't deal with it, couldn't accept that Wesley was broken, couldn't accept that Wesley couldn't help being broken. Simone wasn't that strong, I guess, and she kind of went along with sending him away. Lewis was older and I think just wanted some peace. I suppose it was all about Wesley back then.

"The only one that didn't give up on him, I guess, was Alicia."

I've got to get back to the paper before Sally sends out a search party, or they just say fuck it and hire a new night cops reporter. But with a little encouragement, Clara tells me the rest.

Wesley was eighteen when Alicia was raped, living in a group home somewhere on Meadow Street. Everyone was so upset that it was three days before they realized Wes was missing. It took six months and a private detective to find him, in a jail in Nevada. Apparently, a cop had tried to arrest him, and Wes took a swing at him.

"I guess what happened to Alicia just drove him over the edge. Harper spent a few thousand dollars, I heard, to get him out of there and back home and back on his medication."

Home, Clara explained, wasn't the stately manor where I'd tried to talk with Alicia. Or at least not for very long. Something, she said, would always happen, and Wes would be evicted. He lived in various "homes," and sometimes in his own apartment, depending on how well his current drugs were working and how faithfully he was taking them.

He enrolled at VCU and eventually got a degree, more than I can say for my darling daughter so far, and was hired to work for the law firm of one of Harper's old friends, "probably just clerical stuff, but he had a job."

"Lewis said he lives somewhere over in the Museum District now. He kind of keeps to himself, and she said he hasn't had an episode in more than six years."

"Had an episode" apparently is code for "went batshit." The last "episode," Clara tells us, ended with Lewis and Carl traveling to some small town in Quebec and spending what would be, to me, a lot of money.

"But Lewis says the drugs they have now are so much better than in the old days."

Lewis also confided in Clara that Wesley is spending at least some of his time in their parents' old house, now that they're gone.

"I don't think Lewis is too happy about that," Clara says. "She's afraid it'll make him get into old habits." Like going nuts, I guess. "But they left the house to Alicia, and she didn't seem to mind him staying over.

"It probably passes to Lewis and Carl now, so I don't know what's going to happen. Lewis said they might move back in, try to fix the place up. It's gotten pretty run down."

Run down, I'm thinking, is a relative term.

We're nearing the Prestwould, where I'll drop Clara off and Kate will retrieve her car, when I ask Clara about Lewis.

"Oh," she says, "Lewis is Lewis. Harper always called her his rock, the one he could depend on."

Lewis was the only one of the three who went what you might call the traditional West End route. From what I've seen of some of these tapped-out old Richmond families, one out of three ain't bad.

She graduated in four years from Sweet Briar and married Carl. They have a son who's just gotten into law school at the University of Virginia, a daughter at Sweet Briar and a younger son still at home.

"Wonderful kids," Clara says. "Wonderful family, really. Simone was so proud of them. They're members of the Quarry, too, although I don't see them as much as I used to."

I walk Clara up the steps to the front door, and she gives me a peck on the cheek.

"You know," she says, looking down at Kate, who's waiting for me to take her around back to her car, "what was good once can be good again. Broke doesn't have to stay broke."

"Maybe" is about as far as I'm willing to take that one.

"Well," Kate says, after I've driven her around to the back parking lot and gallantly open her driver's side door for her, "thanks for the ride . . . and all."

"And all? That's a pretty paltry phrase for this afternoon's festivities."

"Hah," she says. It sounds like something between a snort and a laugh. "Festivities. I like that."

"You certainly seemed to."

"I was faking it."

It's time for my own "hah." The former Kate Black, perhaps soon to be the former Kate Ellis, could fake a lot of things—interest in my stories of ill-fated drug deals, tolerance for my perambulations from the straight and narrow, my old Oregon Hill friends, an admiration for my crumbling physique.

What she could not and cannot fake is an orgasm. I remind her of that, and she blushes, pretty much the same way she blushes when she is being vigorously entertained by Mr. Johnson and can't hide it.

"Well," she says, "so I'm a slut."

She gives me a kiss, a real one with all the bells and whistles.

As she reaches to unlock her car door, she says, "But this was an aberration, an anomaly, a one-night—or afternoon—stand. You're a bad habit I can't afford to get hooked on again."

OK. Fair enough.

"But it was good," she concedes, just before she shuts the door on our little time-out from divorce.

Back at the paper, I do a little electronic snooping and get to read Baer's story on the funeral. He wasn't invited to Chez Witt, of course, but he's done a passable job of catching what he would call the zeitgeist. I remember the time Sally called him on that one when he used it in print, in a story about the watermelon festival in Carytown.

"Shit, Mark," she said, "why don't you just come right out and tell them how much smarter you are than they are? People love to be talked down to. Save 'zeitgeist' until you get that job at the *Post*. 'Zeitgeist' and 'watermelon' do not belong in the same story."

It's a blessedly slow night. I call Andi to find out which restaurant she's waitressing at this week, and also try to find out something about her social life with my usual lack of success.

"With this economy," she says, when I wonder aloud how long it'll take her to graduate taking two courses a semester, "why hurry?"

It's hard to argue with that, much as I want to.

About nine thirty, I get a call from Marcus Green.

"Hey," he says. "You still interested in interviewing my client?"

I tell him I'll call him back in thirty seconds.

In the smokers' gulag, I use my cellphone. I explain that I've been taken off the story.

"Man," he says, "those guys take care of their own, don't they?"

Marcus doesn't have to check ESPN to know what the score is. He's been watching game film of West End power brokers for a very long time, looking for tendencies and weaknesses.

I tell him that Mark Baer is going to be covering whatever else happens to Richard Slade.

"My client doesn't want to talk to Mark Baer. He wants to talk to you."

"That's flattering, Marcus."

"Flattering doesn't have shit to do with it. His momma told him about you maybe being his cousin and all."

I opine that maybe I'm making some inroads with Philomena Slade after all.

Marcus Green laughs.

"Well, she's got a pretty good hard-on against all you scoundrels down there. That's what she called y'all the other day, after she threw you out of the car.

"But maybe she thinks you're the best of a bad lot. You being family and all. That still tickles me, by the way. You're about as African-American as Donald Trump."

"Hurts coming from you. You've probably got a butler and a maid."

Green lives along River Road. I've seen his place. He even had a lawn jockey out front for a while. All the white folks out there painted theirs white, about as far as most of them were willing to ride on the tolerance train, so Marcus painted his black, in some kind of twisted attempt at sardonic humor that went over like a fart in a phone booth. He finally gave up after the jockey got stolen three times. The last time, somebody put a love note in his mailbox, calling him a racist cracker and promising more personal and heartfelt retribution.

Marcus harrumphs.

"I'm just a proud black man who's pulled himself up by his bootstraps, overcoming oppression every step on the way."

We both laugh. If the Grand Wizard—or whatever the hell he is—of the Ku Klux Klan offered Marcus Green a nice payday, Marcus would be right there, with that same aggrieved look, fuming over the injustice that awaited his client if a fair and balanced jury didn't save the day.

Still, Marcus Green has helped me, and vice versa. Sometimes, we are aiming in the same direction. Often, neither of us is pure of heart, but sometimes you have to be saved by a scoundrel.

"Yeah," I say, "I'd like very much to talk to your client. Tell him that, if there's some truth to be had, we will get at it."

And I promise him something else. I promise that I'll find a way to get that truth, whatever it might be, into the paper.

It's a promise I hope I can keep.

CHAPTER TEN

Thursday

Peachy Love succeeded me in my first incarnation on night cops. Then, she decided she liked the police end of things better than the newspaper end. She's been a flack for them now for about twelve years. We have an agreement. She's never seen talking to me, except maybe at a group press conference. I never mention her name. But, when either of us knows it's necessary, we talk.

Usually, like today, it's over the phone, although I have been known to make an after-hours house call to Peachy's place in Ginter Park.

"Thought I'd give you a heads-up," she says. I'm still two-thirds asleep. Her voice tells me I'd better wake up fast.

"Yeah?"

"The guy you're checking on? He's going to be a TV star today."

Richard Slade, it turns out, did not sleep tight in his old bed at his mother's house last Friday night. Either that, or his identical twin was in the Kwik-Mart two miles away at three thirty A.M., buying a carton of cigarettes.

"Trust me," Peachy says, "it's him. I saw the tape."

And so, it seems, will everyone in Richmond before the day is out.

I ask her how the surveillance tape got into the hands of one of our local network affiliates.

"Hell if I know. Might have been one of the investigators, might have been the guy at the Kwik-Mart. Doesn't much matter, right now, does it? It'll be on the noon news, though. You can count on that. They've already called the chief, asking for a comment on it."

I thank her and hang up. It's nine thirty. I'd planned to sleep for another hour. I'm supposed to meet Marcus Green at the city jail at one thirty. Now, I'm wondering if I should even bother to go.

Richard Slade might as well be wearing a toe tag already. This just plants him about six feet deeper. I have been accused of having a soft spot in the head for the underdog. But I do expect the underdog not to bite me on the ass with lies and bullshit while I'm trying to help him. A guy who says he slept all night like a baby at his momma's house should not be videotaped at three thirty A.M. buying cigarettes at the Kwik-Mart. It sends the wrong message.

But, there's nothing much to do until I show up for work. Assuming Green doesn't drop the guy like bad meat, I'll be there. It should be entertaining, at least.

There is time, though, before noon, to run a fool's errand.

The guess here is that our local TV news pups didn't bother to call Philomena Slade. Somebody ought to tell her before she hears about it on the news, or from Mark Baer or somebody else calling her for a comment.

By the time I shower, shave and wash down two Krispy Kremes with some of the coffee Custalow kindly left for me, it's ten forty-five, and it's after eleven when I get to Philomena's.

She doesn't seem that glad to see me, our little truce notwithstanding. In the background, I can hear Jamal and Jeroy playing.

"There's something you need to know," I tell her, and she goes silent but leaves the door open about four inches.

When she hears about the surveillance tape, the door opens the rest of the way. She doesn't invite me in, just turns and walks away, defeated.

She sits down at the kitchen table. One of its leaves sags as she puts her elbows on it.

"Not now, Jamal," she tells the twin who wants her to play a child's card game with him.

"Why did he do that?" she says, not really asking me but just the world in general, or maybe God.

I'm thinking the most obvious answer usually is the right one. He went out in the middle of the night because he knew, somehow, that Alicia Parker Simpson always came down a certain street at a certain time every day of the week, and he had some issues that all the forgiveness in the world couldn't wash away.

"I wondered," she says, and now she is talking to me. "I wondered about those cigarettes."

She'd found most of a carton of Kools in his bedroom, and it crossed her mind briefly that she hadn't seen them before Saturday afternoon and didn't remember Richard going out that day.

"A friend came by that morning, a fella he'd known in prison who got out before he did, and I guess I just thought he brought the cigarettes. Richard didn't smoke before he went to jail. I'm hoping he's going to try to quit."

Then she goes silent, perhaps realizing that nicotine is not her son's biggest problem right now.

I tell her I just wanted to let her know, because somebody might be calling her, asking questions.

She looks up, tired-eyed, like she needs to sleep.

"Isn't that what you do?"

I explain that I'm not on the story anymore.

"So what are you doing here?"

I can't come up with a better answer than the one that comes out:

"Because you're family."

She seems to accept this, and I feel certain she's being honest when she says that she never heard anything the night her son took his soon-to-be-infamous ride.

"Guess I sleep more soundly than I realized. Those Ambiens really knock me out."

When I get to the door, she stops me with a slight pressure on my elbow.

"I don't know what kind of evidence they're coming up with," she says, "but I know, just as sure as I'm standing here, that he did not kill that woman. I know that."

I nod and tell her I'll do what I can to find out more. When I wave to her through the screen, the twins are clinging to her dress.

I get to the jail at one fifteen. I am kind of surprised when Marcus Green shows up five minutes later. Kate's not with him.

"Well," he says to me, not appearing the least bit daunted, "we've got some work to do."

I suggest that all the work in the world might not save his client.

"Aw," he says, "I've had worse cases than this."

"That you won?"

"Let's just wait and see," he says.

Maybe it's my imagination, but the jailer who escorts us to the interview room seems to be smirking. Half of Richmond must know by now about Richard Slade's little after-hours run.

Slade, when we get to the room, doesn't look that much different than he did when he went free ten days ago, but I'm thinking he's going to be a little hard to read. He's had most of his life so far to work on keeping his true self hidden.

I can't tell, until he speaks, that he knows.

"I heard about the tape," is all he says.

"Would've been nice if I'd heard about all this somewhere other than the TV," Marcus says.

"I didn't know . . ." he says, then stops and looks off, focusing on some point beyond the wall behind us.

"Well," Marcus says, "you better start truthin' right now, or get yourself another lawyer."

This gets Slade's attention. He looks, for a fraction of a second, like I imagine that scared teenager did back in 1983. Other than his mother, he knows Marcus Green is all he's got. He might not know, as I do, that his lawyer would dump him like a box of cat litter if it begins to look like Marcus Green's best interests aren't being served. I've seen him do it.

I've been mostly a fly on the wall so far, waiting to pick up what shit I can out of this.

Slade seems to notice me for the first time.

"So you're the white sheep of the family," he says.

I explain it all as quick as I can, including the part about how I'm not really on the story anymore. Richard Slade might or might not believe me, but he and I both know he's not in a position to alienate anyone who has a better than twenty-to-one shot at saving his ass. He probably knows that a distant cousin who might or might not ever write anything else about the mess he's in might be the best shot he has.

"Anyhow," Marcus says, getting the conversation back to where it might do someone some good, "tell it."

Slade grimaces.

"Bump came by, and he wanted me and him to go for a ride."

"He came by when?"

"It was about two in the morning."

"He just knocked on your momma's door at two A.M.?"

Slade is quiet for a few seconds, and I can hear the gears shifting, like he's doing a little self-editing. Marcus and I exchange a glance.

"Well," he says, "it wasn't quite like that."

"What I'm here for," Marcus says, raising his voice the way he might pounce on a vulnerable witness who's just identified his client, "is the truth. T-R-U-T-H. Not a bunch of bullshit. The truth."

"OK, OK." Slade holds his cuffed hands up. "I ran into him that afternoon. I was just out walking, and he sees me and pulls over. He said he was going to work, wouldn't get off till one in the morning, but he'd come by and get me. We'd go down to the docks, drink a couple of beers, catch up, you know?"

"I don't know anything," Marcus Green says, his arms crossed. "Educate me. Start off by telling me who Bump is."

Bump Freeman, Slade explains, was his friend when they were growing up.

"Hadn't seen him in twenty-eight years," he says, which makes me wonder why Mr. Freeman never visited him, but sometimes friends can be fickle. If anybody understands that, it's Richard Slade.

"He was with me that night."

At first, I don't understand, and then I do.

"At the Quarry?"

He nods his head.

"I think he wanted to try to tell me about, you know, what happened."

"What happened," Marcus says, "is he and your other so-called friends sold your ass out."

Slade shrugs.

"We were kids. Cops came after me like they did him, I'd have done the same thing."

I can tell that Marcus, who is the type to redress old wrongs instead of forgiving them, isn't exactly buying this.

Slade says the plan was for his old buddy Bump Freeman, whom he hadn't seen since Bump was helping send him to prison, to come by, and they'd go catch up.

"I knew he'd be by about two, so I just set the alarm for one thirty. Then I sat on the front steps and waited."

According to Slade, Bump had picked up a couple of 40s, and they went down to the dock. They sat in the car, sipping malt liquor and looking out at the river with the car's heat going, and they caught up.

"Did anybody see you?" Marcus asks him.

"Naw. Man, it was freezing out there. Nobody to see us."

"Bump never visited your ass in prison?"

Slade shakes his head.

"He said he was too ashamed."

"Hell," Marcus mutters, "he should've been."

On the way back, Slade wanted some cigarettes. He went in and Bump stayed in the car.

"We were back to my momma's house by four thirty, at the latest. I swear."

Swear all you want, I'm thinking.

"Did anybody see you get out of Bump's car and go inside?" Marcus asks him.

Slade shakes his head again.

"I don't think so."

Alicia Parker Simpson was shot around five fifteen. That time of morning, you could get there from Philomena's house in fifteen minutes, maybe ten. Even if Richard Slade did what he said he did, up to the time he came back with his Kools from the Kwik-Mart, he had time to go out again, either by himself or with the ever-helpful Bump, and wait for his accuser. Maybe Bump had visited him in prison after all. Maybe he was helping to settle an old score, make up for not being there twenty-eight years ago.

And about the only person who can even begin to vouch for Slade, it appears, is the redoubtable Bump Freeman.

Where, Marcus asks him, does Bump live?

Slade tells him that he lives "somewhere over by the school," which turns out to be about two blocks away.

"So you went back inside when you got back?"

"Yeah. I was beat. I went straight to bed."

I've got a question of my own.

"What about the guy who came by to see you that morning? Your momma said some guy who was at Greensville with you stopped by."

He looks surprised.

"Oh," he says, "you mean Shooter Sheets. Yeah, he wanted to wish me good luck, on getting out and all."

Shooter Sheets, Slade explains, had gotten out of prison a couple of years ago and was working as an auto mechanic now.

I ask him why he was called Shooter, and he just looks at me like I'm the biggest dumb-ass in the world.

"So," Marcus says, "you went out in the middle of the night and got yourself a screen test at the Kwik-Mart, and nobody saw you come or go, other than some damn Indian clerk, and you spent time earlier in the day with an ex-con named Shooter."

"I know how it looks," Slade says. "But can't you find Bump? He'll vouch for what I said."

I know what Marcus Green is thinking. Even if the upstanding Mr. Freeman is willing to go against form and step up for his old friend, who's going to believe him? I'm hoping that, when Bump Freeman got home at the alleged hour of four thirty or so, he woke somebody up.

And what was to keep Richard Slade from heading back out again, or getting into somebody else's car? Maybe he just let Bump do it, or maybe this guy Shooter.

Any way you look at it, there's not a lot of positive takeaway from having the whole world find out that you lied about where you were on the night that the woman you had every reason to hate was murdered.

I've listened to a lot of con jobs by cons, ex- and otherwise. If you're on the cops beat, sometimes they fixate on the guy who wrote all those bad things about them. And then, when they're convicted, they try to stay in touch, as if a few bylines have bonded our asses for life.

It's funny, but they don't ever seem resentful. In most cases, they just seem to want to convince you that they didn't do it, even after the police and the judge and jury and everyone else, myself included, is sure of the opposite.

It is always, I learned early on, wise not to respond to the eight-page, handwritten jailhouse letters. These guys have a lot of time on their hands, and they're looking for a Best Friend Forever on the outside. Then, when they get out, they can look you up, which is not a thing you might necessarily want to happen.

Richard Slade never did that. Other than the occasional letter from his mother, he was out of sight, out of mind. And yet, he kind of won me over in the ten days since he was released. Until today, he seemed like the closest thing to an innocent victim I've seen go through our penal system—a guy who was locked away for damn near half his life and then harbored no grudges when he got out, just wanted to sit on a front porch with no bars on it and savor freedom.

Well, I've been done in by gut feelings before.

As we're leaving, Slade puts his hand on my arm.

"Help me," is all he says.

I tell him I'll see what I can do. The way he looks at me, I can tell that he sees what a lost cause I think he is. I look away.

On the way out, Marcus Green doesn't say much.

I try to crack the silence a little as we're walking down the steps.

"So, do you think he did it?"

He stops and turns to me.

"If I did," he says, "I sure as hell wouldn't tell you about it. He's my client."

"But you told him that if he wasn't telling the truth, he'd have to get another lawyer."

Marcus frowns and then nods.

"Yeah. I said that."

"And you didn't drop him."

Marcus starts walking away. With all the street noise, I barely hear him say, "Not yet."

CHAPTER ELEVEN

The newsroom is humming when I get there, or as close to humming as it gets without typewriter keys as background music. Sarah looks up when I walk by.

"Some story, huh?" she says.

"Yeah. Where's Baer?"

She motions toward Wheelie's office. I see the back of Baer's head, nodding up and down like a Bobblehead doll. Whatever Wheelie's telling him, he seems to be in complete agreement.

Then I notice another head, to the left of Baer's and much less animated. I take a few steps over and see that our publisher has graced us with his ghostly presence.

Wheelie and Grubby. Grubby doesn't descend into the newsroom except on rare occasions. I'm guessing that the latest bombshell in the Alicia Simpson story has led to some cages being rattled. Maybe even Grubby's cage.

I slip away to get a cup of coffee before anyone sees me, in case they want to invite me to the party. Wheelie's office gets awfully small when there are more than two people in there, especially if one of them is the publisher.

When I come back, Grubby's gone back upstairs and Baer's been freed.

I'm checking with the cops to see what mayhem has occurred during the past fourteen hours when I feel Baer's presence. He likes to hover, and he's been known to read what's on other people's screens, like a runner on second stealing signs from the catcher. I have an urge to brush him back.

"Willie," he says when I reluctantly hang up. "Can you help me? Nobody knows more about this than you do."

One of Baer's strong points, and one that might eventually earn him a job in Washington or New York, or at least Atlanta or Philadelphia, is that he can lick ass when the occasion calls for it. If you've been around him long, you know that it's only temporary. You know that, if the situation were reversed, he wouldn't piss on you to douse the flames if you were on fire. But, it works, for a while.

Baer can't get anyone to talk to him. After TV was fed the news that Richard Slade was out and about in the wee hours before the murder, the cops stopped talking. I know for a fact that Marcus Green isn't talking to Baer, as a small favor to me that I'm sure I'll be repaying with twenty percent interest, compounded weekly, and he sure as hell isn't letting his client speak to him. I'm pretty sure that Philomena Slade would kick his ass around the block a time or two if he showed up in her neighborhood, just because he was from the paper.

"I'll make you a deal," I tell him after he's made his pitch.

Baer, I am sure, has complete and unfettered access to Lewis Witt, and probably to brother Wesley, too. Not even the intervention of Clara Westbrook can get me so far up that road.

"You're going to go see Lewis Witt, right?"

"Well, yeah. Matter of fact, I'm going over there this afternoon."

"Take me with you."

Baer is stumped. He doesn't want me to weasel back into this story that's been dropped into his lap.

He frowns and then realizes he doesn't know what the tit for his tat is.

"What do I get?"

"I'll get you an interview with Philomena Slade."

I doubt this is possible, but I'm pretty sure Baer doesn't know whether he can get me past the front door at the Witts' abode, either. We're just two guys holding low-card pairs and bluffing. He's got to get something from the other side to go with everything the Witts are more than eager to tell him. I really, really want to talk to Lewis Witt.

"Aren't you supposed to be off this story?"

"I just need to scratch an itch," I tell him.

He thinks about it and then shrugs.

"OK with me. I don't know if she'll let you in, though."

I tell him I'll count on his boyish charm.

"But I really need to talk to Mrs. Slade."

I nod my head.

We're off an hour later, after I've done a couple of shorts on people who were only robbed and shot but not killed. We wouldn't even put the robbery bit in the paper, but it was VCU students, forced to relinquish their cellphones and cash at gunpoint. Crime against middle-class kids, probably white, will always sell papers. I think about Andi, walking all over the Fan in the dead of night, probably talking on the phone or texting, not paying attention.

I tell Sally that I'll be back in time to check on any late-night misdeeds among the populace.

The sun is threatening to set on us by the time we get to the Witts' place. Baer rings the doorbell. They're expecting him, but certainly not me. I'm hoping maybe Lewis Witt has put some of her animosity toward me on the back burner. When we're shown in, the look in her eyes tells me I'm mistaken.

"What is he doing here?" she asks Baer.

I tell her that today's events have made me think twice about Richard Slade. What I say has enough truth in it that I don't blush saying it.

"Well," she says, "I hope you know now what kind of animal the criminal justice system has turned loose on us. A little late, though."

I swallow and nod.

She stands back, silently accepting my non-apology and not bothering to ask why it takes two reporters to interview her.

She stops after a few steps.

"Is your, ah, ex-wife still defending that bastard?"

I tell her that she was helping Marcus Green, but that she's having second thoughts now.

Lewis Witt's nose wrinkles at the mention of Marcus.

"I should hope so," she says.

There's no one else visible, although I can hear music somewhere in the recesses of the Witt home, which seems about four times too big for the three people living there now.

Baer tells Lewis that we're just trying to get the story straight, that we want to do a piece on the Simpson family and its impact on Richmond through the years.

The Simpson family's impact on Richmond, as far as I can learn, is to have made as much money as possible getting suckers like me hooked on nicotine, then giving some of it back to the symphony and the fine arts museum. But Lewis seems to be more or less buying Baer's explanation for our presence, and she spends a couple of hours regaling us with more family history than anyone should be expected to endure. I get through it by drinking three cups of coffee and asking an occasional question of my own, and finally we get to 1983 and the Philadelphia Quarry.

Baer asks most of the questions. Lewis was twenty-two, just graduated from college, when it happened.

"I was down in Atlanta, interning there for a PR firm, trying to decide what to do with the rest of my life," she says.

"Daddy called me and said something had happened to Alicia. I didn't really hear the whole story until I got back, and then Momma had to tell me."

She abruptly quit her job, such as it was, and returned home.

"They needed me," she says. "And Wes sure as hell wasn't any help."

Baer and I have to agree that whatever she says about Wesley's disappearance after "the incident" can only be used for background.

He could hardly have picked a worse time to disappear, everyone agreed.

"Daddy was not that inclined to look for him, but Momma and I persuaded him to hire a detective. It was sometime in October before he showed up in Nevada. We never did find out what happened to the car."

"Where's he staying now?" I ask. As with my other questions, she looks at Baer when she answers.

"He's got a place in the Museum District, but we're letting him stay at my parents' home, for now."

The way she says "for now" makes it quite clear that it is a markedly different time span than "forever."

Baer asks her if we can speak with Wesley. She says she doesn't think that would be a good idea, that Alicia's death has hit him very hard.

I'm thinking, Wes is forty-six years old. Surely he can make his own decisions.

But I bite my tongue and then ask her if Alicia had ever talked about that night.

"If she did," Lewis Witt says, giving Baer the laser death stare she means for me, "I certainly wouldn't share that with you. We are not the kind of people to air our dirty laundry."

No doubt Giles Whitehurst has assured her that no one from the paper will be asking any rude questions.

I shut up before I get both me and Baer thrown out. Carl Witt comes in. From the look on his wife's face, he wasn't supposed to do that. He offers us drinks and we decline. We play a little verbal badminton for a few more minutes, and it's time to go.

Back in the car, Baer wants to know what I think.

"About?"

"About what Lewis Witt just said."

"I'd say she's had a rough week. Write the story and move on."

When we get back to the paper, there's a message on my phone. Ninety seconds, the recorded female voice says. Damn,

I hate those. Ninety-second calls are usually from poor suckers who want you to do a story on how they've been fucked over by life through no fault of their own and want somebody to write about it.

This one, though, is a little different.

"Hello? This is Susan Winston-Jones?"

It takes me a few seconds to remember who Susan Winston-Jones is.

"You know, we met after the funeral yesterday?"

The late Alicia Simpson's friend seems to be playing *Jeopardy*, framing everything in the form of a question, but after she rambles a bit, she cuts to the chase.

"I'd like you to give me a call, at your convenience. I think I have something that might be of interest to you, about Alicia?"

She has my attention.

I go into one of our conference rooms and call the number she gave me.

She tells me to call her Bitsy, and then spends a few minutes telling me what a fine person her late friend was.

"She was a little fragile, but, you know, she always wanted to do the right thing."

I'm wondering if Richard Slade would necessarily agree with that.

"Here's the thing," Bitsy says, just as I'm about to tell her to get on with it. "Alicia was writing something."

"Writing something?"

"You know, like her memoirs or something? But she wouldn't let me see it. She told me, sometime early last week, that she'd let me read it when she was finished, and she said she was nearly finished."

"Do you have any idea," I ask, "what it was about?"

There's a pause.

"Kind of," Bitsy says at last. "She said that it would—how did she put it?—'finally tell the truth.' She said she'd finally be able to sleep nights."

"But you don't know what she did with it?"

"I asked Lewis about it, the day of the funeral. She said she didn't know anything about it, and that there wasn't anything in the desk Alicia was using, but that she would check and see if there was anything on her computer."

I ask her if she knows anything else about Alicia Parker Simpson's "memoirs," and she says she doesn't, "but there was something there, something she wanted to get out."

"Did Lewis seem like she knew about it at all before you mentioned it?"

"Well, she tried to hide it, but I think she did know. She acted kind of funny, kind of flustered, which is not Lewis, trust me. She did seem surprised, but I couldn't tell if it was because Alicia was writing something or because I knew about it."

One of the news editors and a reporter open the conference room door. I wave them away, and the editor frowns and mouths that he has the room reserved. I hold up five fingers.

"Anyhow, I wanted you to know about it. In case there was something there, you know?"

I ask Bitsy why exactly she wanted me to know about a missing manuscript that was probably just a middle-aged socialite's bow to Narcissus. Well, I didn't put it quite that bluntly, but she got the message.

"Because of something she said."

I resist the urge to ask. Better to let the silence draw it out.

"It was the same conversation where she told me about her memoirs, so it must have been Monday week, because it was the same day they released that man. And you know what she said?"

Silence.

"She said, 'Thank God. He's suffered enough. I'm the one that ought to be suffering.' And then she shut up about it and never mentioned it again. I meant to talk with her about it, but I never had the chance."

Bitsy's voice breaks a little. I tell her I'm sorry about her friend, and that I'll look into it, although I have no earthly idea how.

I ask her, before I hang up, to call me if she remembers anything else.

Outside, having avoided the lethal stare of the editor who had reserved space in the conference room at the time I was interviewing Bitsy Winston-Jones, I warm myself from the heat of the Camel I'm forced to smoke alfresco. I'm trying to figure if there's anything out there that I should be chasing. Richard Slade looks as guilty as sin, to me and everyone else. Even if he didn't do the deed twenty-eight years ago, he sure as hell is the prime suspect for Alicia Simpson's murder. What difference could a manuscript, missing or otherwise, make?

Only one thing to do, I decide at last: Blog.

They want us to blog every day, like flossing. With me, it's a sometimes thing. I still don't hold some unedited crap offered to our former readers on the Internet in the same high regard I reserve for the printed, paper-and-ink word. And I don't care if we cut down all the trees in Oregon to do it.

Still, it has its place. When you don't know shit, but you've heard some pretty juicy gossip, it's a good place to fling it, see if any of it sticks. I've gotten some pretty good tips, actually, by slinging stuff up against the electronic wall.

So, back inside and, with no murders to sully our fair city so far tonight, I blog.

"Is there a story behind the story of Alicia Parker Simpson's tragic death?" I muse. I love to muse. "Is it true that she was working on her memoirs at the time of her death, and that those memoirs have mysteriously disappeared?" (Nothing ever just disappears, it mysteriously disappears.) I blog on, mentioning Richard Slade's unfortunate bad judgment in being out in the wee hours before Alicia was murdered, even throw in the fact that an old friend might be able to vouch for his whereabouts, if that old friend can be found.

It goes on for a few paragraphs. Then I hit the "publish" button and wait to see what happens next.

Sally Velez, who actually reads some of the crap we put on our blogs, comes by an hour or so later.

"Jesus Christ," she says. "Grubby is going to barbecue you."

Well, I said I'd cede the story to Baer. I didn't say I wouldn't blog about it. But I doubt if our publisher will appreciate that fine distinction.

CHAPTER TWELVE

Friday

Custalow is in the kitchen, getting breakfast. I'm sitting by the living room window, overlooking Monroe Park, with my head halfway out, sending my secondhand smoke in the direction of the pigeons and squirrels.

"You going to keep that window open much longer?" Custalow asks as he walks in. It is late January, and even the joy of nicotine is diminished somewhat by the fact that I'm freezing my ass off. Abe, munching on a bagel, is only getting the down side.

"Doesn't look good for Richard Slade," he says as he sits down. He's carrying the paper, reading the front page.

I agree with him.

"I still can't see it," he says.

"Can't see what?"

"Nobody I knew at Greensville ever thought he did it to start with, you know, rape that girl. And he was the most peaceable guy you'd ever want to meet. Course, he was pushing forty when I met him. Maybe he was wild when he was young."

"Weren't we all."

Custalow checks his watch.

"The thing is," he says as he gets up, "he spent twenty-eight years behind bars. He did everything right. And then it turns out he really didn't do it. So, I'm thinking, is it possible the first crime Richard Slade ever committed was a well-planned execution?"

Not that well-planned, I remind him, but Custalow does have a point. It's why I haven't given up on the fact that there's a story here beyond the one we've spread across the front page this morning. I've checked, and Slade didn't seem to have any kind of record before he was arrested for raping Alicia Simpson.

"Maybe he was a little pissed off," I suggest, always the devil's faithful advocate, "spending half his life in prison for something he didn't do. That'd do it for me."

"Maybe," Custalow says, "but he didn't seem like that kind. You know, he wrote his mother every week, read the Bible all the time, led prayer groups. You can fake that stuff for a while, but not for twenty-eight years."

Custalow heads for the door.

"Hey," I call to him, "the radiator pipes are still clanging. Maybe you ought to get some outside help."

"I'm on it," he says, fixing me with a stare that would surely qualify as baleful.

Not fifteen minutes after he leaves, the phone rings. Foolishly, I answer it.

It's Sally.

"Mr. Grubbs wants to see you," she says, and the fact that she doesn't call him "Grubby" tells me he must be right there by her desk.

"About what?"

I'm pretty sure I know what. The blog. Probably wasn't one of my better ideas. I may have used up whatever stay-out-of-the-unemployment-line points I've ever earned.

She ignores my question.

"He wants you here in an hour."

That would be ten o'clock, about four hours before I start getting paid.

"Sally," I tell her, "I know he's standing right there beside you, making you call me. Just say 'All right' if that's so."

She pauses for a couple of seconds, then says it.

"OK. Tell him I'm on my way."

She says "All right" again and I hang up.

It's only ten blocks up Franklin Street from the Prestwould to the paper. It's a nice, compact little world. I pass the YMCA, where a better person would stop for a workout on the way to the office, and the city library, and only a block beyond the paper is Penny Lane, where everybody knows my name. Who could ask for anything more?

I'd hate to mess this up. If I get fired, there isn't anything else I can do that's legal that would pay nearly what I'm drawing now.

Still, give me truth serum and I'd tell you that I don't regret being the fly in the ointment, the turd in the punch bowl, refusing to write off Richard Slade. Most of my best stories were the ones somebody told me not to write. If I took orders better, I'd still be drinking and hobnobbing with our state legislators, where all the crimes are legal, instead of spending my late middle age chasing police cars.

It's not much after ten when I get there.

I go straight to the fourth floor, where Sandy McCool greets me and tells me Mr. Grubbs will be with me shortly. I know better than to expect Sandy, longtime friend and Grubby's executive assistant, to be The Weather Channel and tell me just how big a shitstorm I've stirred up. Sandy's a good woman, but she takes her job seriously.

Five minutes later, she tells me he'll see me.

I knock on Grubby's door and he says to come in. He doesn't even bother to get up from his desk.

"Sit," he says.

"Willie," he begins, leaning forward, "what part of 'Let Baer have the Richard Slade story' did you not understand?"

I start to protest that I haven't written a word about Slade in the last three days' papers. He puts up one of his hands to stop me.

"You blogged about it, and from what I can tell, about half the city's read that. You went to the funeral. You went to the city jail and talked to him, you and Marcus Green."

I don't know how he found out about that last part, but it's not that big a town.

"Do you know I've been on the phone with Giles Whitehurst? He called me at seven this morning. He doesn't want to fire your ass, Willie. He wants to fire my ass, because he assumes I don't have any control over this newspaper, over what our reporters do."

I'm truly sorry for that. James H. Grubbs is a back-stabbing corporate climber who sold his journalistic soul for an MBA, but I did promise to stay off the story, and I haven't. I don't want to make anyone the recipient of a seven A.M. phone call from the chairman of the board, not even Grubby.

There isn't much to do except try to convince our publisher that there was a good reason for doing what I did, that there is that tiny chance that we're putting the hanging before the trial.

Even as I'm telling Grubby what I know about Slade, I realize that it's weak as water. My ex-con housemate and friend knew him in prison and doesn't think he's capable of something so heinous. There's a guy out there, according to Slade, who will corroborate his story. Slade has never, to anyone's knowledge, ever assaulted another human being, let alone murdered one.

When I tell him about Susan Winston-Jones and the alleged missing diary, journal, memoirs, whatever the fuck it was, Grubby seems only mildly more interested than before. I catch him sneaking a peak at his watch.

"We have to do something, Willie," he says.

"We?"

"OK. I. I have to do something. You're suspended."

"For how long?"

"Let's say two weeks. Two weeks without pay."

It doesn't really bother me as much as it should. Two weeks won't break me. Quite.

"This isn't going to look good on my résumé. How am I ever going to get a job at the *Washington Post* with this blemish on my reputation?"

Grubby almost thinks I'm serious, then nearly smiles at the idea of the *Post* hiring a fifty-something almost-white guy whose reputation already has more stains than a two-year-old's bib at a spaghetti supper.

I figure there's not much to lose, so I tell Grubby that the presumed-guilty Mr. Slade probably is my cousin.

"So you've not been exactly unbiased about this."

I concede that this might possibly be the case, but that I do believe the story hasn't been fully told yet. I add that it doesn't seem like Giles Whitehurst is an impartial bystander either.

"Oh, he's definitely not a bystander," Grubby says.

We both know there's a whole herd of sacred cows out in Windsor Farms, and I've been trying to tip one of them over.

I have to ask one more thing, though, even as Grubby is reaching for his coat, no doubt due somewhere else in five minutes.

"I promised to help Baer. Do you want me to do that?"

I don't ever really want to help Baer. I think our publisher and I both know that.

"If you want to, but it's on your own time. The paper does not back or condone anything you do connected to this story. That is our official stance."

"But what I do on my own time is my business, right?"

He pauses and sighs.

"Right."

Another pause.

"Leave it alone, Willie. I don't know why, but this has become Giles Whitehurst's burning desire, that we get this story on the straight and narrow. No diversions, no side streets. Come back in two weeks and start with a clean slate."

I say nothing, but I've got to think even Grubby is smart enough to know that telling me to leave a story alone is like waving a pork chop in front of a pit bull.

I get off the elevator at the second floor. Baer is at his desk all fresh and alert. I realize I have a free day. Free two weeks, for that matter. Free of pay, but free nonetheless. I don't do well when I slip the bonds of employment, though. I wonder who's going to get the choice assignment of night cops for the next fortnight.

I decide I might as well make a mildly honest effort at giving young Mr. Baer what I promised.

"You wanted an interview with Richard Slade's mother."

He looks up, either surprised to see me so early or shocked at my appearance. Didn't have time to shave.

"Yeah. Yeah, definitely. But . . ." he hesitates and lowers his voice. "But don't, you know, don't mention that we're going out there. I'm not supposed to be doing this. I think they just want me to let it drop, everything after Slade's arrest, other than the piece on the Simpson family."

I explain to young Baer that I'm totally aware of the repercussions of pursuing the rest of the story with too much vigor.

"Suspended?" he says. "Just for that blog?"

Baer is weighing in his devious mind the pluses and minuses of coming with me to Philomena Slade's house, consequences be damned. He wants to please, but he wants something big, something that'll move him one step closer to the top of a profession that's becoming as relevant as the Pony Express.

The urge to get ahead outweighs his fear of incurring Grubby's wrath, as I thought it might.

"But you're not getting paid," he says.

"It keeps me off the streets."

We get to Philomena's a little after noon.

"What do you want now?" she asks me.

I introduce her to my friend, Mark Baer, who is unnaturally courteous, the way he is when he wants something, and explain that we've talked to Richard down at the jail and want to work with Marcus Green to see what we can do about telling her son's side of the story.

She doesn't really buy this, but she's a little bit grateful to me, I think, for giving her a heads-up on Richard's unfortunate Kwik-Mart video.

The twins are eating lunch in the background, but come in to check out the latest white guy. I'm thinking there haven't been many white folks in Philomena's house, and probably the ones who were there didn't bring good news.

I tell Philomena that I'm taking a couple of weeks off to do some snooping around on my own, and that Baer is going to be working on whatever we write about her son from now on.

"But you said you were going to do it," she says, obviously not as taken with Baer as he'd like her to be. She has good instincts.

"I'm still going to be looking into it, but just behind the scenes."

"Behind the scenes," she repeats. She's sitting on a somewhat worn couch in the living room, with the sound turned down on the TV. "They didn't fire you, did they?"

I tell her I'm on a leave of absence, then try to give her what reassurance I can.

"Philomena," I say, "I'm going to be checking into it, whether they pay me to or not."

"They don't want you all to write anything about my son, except what a bad man he is. Do they?"

My silence is all the answer she needs.

"You all better go," she says quietly. When Baer tries to sweet-talk her into changing her mind, I see the look in her eyes and gently guide him out the door. The twins follow us with unblinking eyes.

When we get back to the car, Baer stops to fish in his pocket for his keys.

"What happened there? I thought we were going to interview her."

I look back at the little rancher, sure we're being watched, by Momma Phil, her charges and probably half the neighborhood.

"She's just figured out what the score is," I tell him. This is probably not exactly true. I'm thinking Philomena Slade knew the score of this particular game a long time ago, when her son was arrested for raping a white girl from the right side of the tracks.

I get in and, after a few seconds, Baer does the same. We screech away, or as much as you can peel rubber with one of our aging, anemic company cars. Baer, the model of charm a few minutes ago, seems pissed.

"You said you'd get me an interview with her."

"I said I'd try. I'll try again."

But I don't think Momma Phil is ever going to open that door to me again, unless I'm by myself. And maybe not even then.

I'll make my peace with her. I want to. But for now, Baer is going to have to be satisfied with me picking up the tab for lunch at the Red Door.

Penny Lane whispers my name as Baer parks the car. For distraction, I go with him upstairs to the newsroom. He walks a couple of steps ahead of me, sulking like a two-year-old despite his free lunch.

Sarah Goodnight beckons me.

"Thanks a lot," she says, looking almost as pouty as Baer.

"What?"

"I'm on night cops for two weeks."

Sarah knows the basics of what I do. Out of curiosity and a desire to learn all she can, she has ridden with me a couple of times. This is her reward.

"What about your regular beat?" They have Sarah writing features and also let her do an occasional turn covering the General Assembly, which is in high season now.

"Oh, Wheelie said to see if I could manage to sneak in a few GA stories on the side. He said, and I quote, 'You're young. You can sleep later.' "

She's mimicking Wheelie loudly enough that I can hear Jackson, sitting ten feet away, snickering.

"The only good news is, I don't have to do any more of those damn Sense of Place stories."

Wheelie would never pull that crap on an older reporter. Chuck Apple covers cops the nights I'm off, but Chuck's covering city schools, and I'm sure that when he told Wheelie he couldn't be two places at the same time, Wheelie just smiled and backed away.

"Oh," Sarah says, realizing that she might not be the only one having a bad newspaper day, "I'm sorry, about the suspension and all."

Ah, callow youth.

I tell her not to worry, that I'll walk her through it. Plus, night cops isn't quite as fraught with adventure in January. People are not as quick-triggered in January as they are in July.

She thanks me. No problem, I tell her. I've got nothing but time.

I drive over to Oregon Hill, just to make sure Peggy's place hasn't burned down. Nobody answers my knock, but when I try the door, it's open. I find Peggy and Awesome Dude sitting in the kitchen, a roach lying in the ashtray between them. Neither one of them notices me at first. Then, Awesome sees me and jumps half a foot. Usually, when people appear suddenly in Awesome's world, they don't mean him any good. Peggy and Les have taken him in, but I'm thinking that, drug-wise, this is somewhat like housing gasoline and matches together.

"Dude," he says, settling back into his purple haze, "you scared the shit out of me."

"Don't you ever knock?" my mother asks by way of greeting.

"Has all that dope impaired your hearing?"

She tells me to show some respect, which cracks both of us up.

"That was too bad about Philomena's boy," she says when she stops coughing. "Looks like he's just about done for."

I tell her that we'll have to wait and see.

I ask her where Les is. He's taking a nap, something he's only started doing lately. Maybe it comes with old age or dementia. He's still a bear, though, not much diminished physically since I first met him.

"Aren't you supposed to be at work?" she asks when she finally focuses enough to read the clock on the wall.

I explain why I'm at leisure.

"So somebody, some big shot over in Windsor Farms, wants you off the case. Same as it ever was. Money talks, bullshit walks."

"Yeah," Awesome kicks in. "I heard the other day on TV about how the middle class is just disappearing. Ain't no hope for the little man."

I keep my smile inside. Neither Peggy nor Awesome has, in their adult lives, risen to what the world might call "middle class." Peggy's still renting. Awesome might be sleeping in a cardboard box or a homeless shelter, spending his days at the downtown public library, without my addled mother's benevolence.

Peggy offers me a beer, which I accept. When I start to light a cigarette, she tells me I'll have to smoke it outside. Incredible.

"Them Simpsons are strange," Awesome offers more or less out of left field.

I ask him if he knows them socially.

Awesome sees that I'm kidding and smiles. He seems to have a tooth or two less than the last time I saw him, but maybe it's just my imagination.

"Nah," he says, "but I knew Wes."

"Alicia's brother?"

"She the murdered girl? Yeah. Anyhow, Wes, he used to hang out sometimes down by Texas Beach."

According to Awesome Dude, Wesley Simpson, during his stay at the "retreat" where his family parked him, had slipped away on more than one occasion.

"He said he didn't like it there, that those people were—what did he call them?—vulgarians."

"He must be really tore up about his sister, though."

I tell Awesome that I assume anyone would be "tore up" about something like this.

"Yeah," he says, "but she was the only one he had any use for. He used to talk awful about his momma and daddy, and the older sister—he said she just thought he was a loser. He called her a West End bitch.

"He said Alicia was the one that looked out for him. Called her his angel. He was pretty wacked out. A couple of times, the cops came and got him. He was scarin' the tourists."

"The tourists," I've learned from Awesome, is how the people who consider themselves the legitimate residents of Texas Beach, ensconced in their makeshift tents and boxes in the thicket above the river when the weather will permit, refer to the swimmers, kayakers and tubers who come down to the little sandy spit to play in the fecally enhanced water of the James.

"But even when he was wacked out," Awesome says, "he thought a lot of Alicia. He said he owed her, but he wasn't ever going to be able to pay her back."

We chat for a while, then Les comes out, rubbing his eyes.

"What's for breakfast?" he asks. Then, he looks at the clock, which tells him it's half past four.

"Oh, yeah," he says.

Peggy's little makeshift family gets by. Usually, at least one of them has a grip on reality. Les has taken care of my mother, and now she's taking care of him. I know from experience that Peggy, for any faults she might have, looks after her own. And she and Les both consider Awesome "their own" now. He sometimes disappears for a few days at a time, maybe missing his old friends who can only find shelter under government- and charity-supported roofs. But he always comes back.

I talk to Les a little about the upcoming baseball season. An ex-ballplayer himself, he can tell you who won every World Series from 1941 to sometime in the late sixties, although he might forget where Peggy's house is at the end of one of his occasional walkabouts.

When I leave, I look back in the fading light and see them all sitting there side-by-side on the living room couch, watching *Dr. Phil* or some such shit, with their popcorn, beer and dope. Just like a real family.

I call Kate on my cellphone. She's still allowed to use Bartley, Bowman and Bush's offices while she's doing her little Richard Slade sabbatical. I tell the receptionist that I'd like to speak with Kate Black, then correct myself. Must be some kind of Freudian slip.

To my surprise, she answers.

"So," I ask, "is Richard Slade a lost cause?"

"I don't think so. Besides, even if he was, you know how much I love lost causes. I married you, didn't I?"

"Yeah. But that's one you had to run up the white flag on."

"Touché. But you have to admit, I gave it my best shot."

I resist the urge to tell her that I wish she'd tried harder. I can hear the clickety-click of fingers on keyboard. Kate, always the overachiever, is multitasking.

"So where were you yesterday? I thought maybe Marcus was on his own."

She sighs and lowers her voice.

"BB&B is not too happy with me right now," she says. "I think somebody above my pay grade doesn't want me to get involved."

I note that this is quite possible. People trying to help Richard Slade seem to be running into a lot of stone walls, mostly hidden behind boxwoods, covered with ivy and smelling like old money when you smash into them face-first.

"They suspended you?" she says. "How can they do that?"

I remind her that they can do any damn thing they want, just like BB&B can.

"Anyhow," she says, "I'm still working with Marcus, pro bono. I can't even talk about Richard Slade around here."

"Which is why I can barely hear you right now."

"Right."

I tell her about my little slipup with the receptionist, since I'm sure she'll hear about it anyhow.

"Funny," she says, but she doesn't sound amused. "Willie, that ship has already left the dock."

I want to mention that it made landfall briefly in Willieland a couple of days ago, but that would be tacky.

I have a couple of beers with Custalow back at the old home place, explaining my employment situation yet again.

He advises me to watch my ass. Neither one of us can afford to rent this place on one salary, at least not for long.

I ask him if he thinks I should drop Richard Slade like the hot potato he is.

He stops with a sandwich inches from his mouth.

"Hell, no. Not unless you think he did it. Remember the WWSD Oath."

Despite the fact that Custalow has been living with me for a while, and despite the fact that I see McGonnigal and Andy Peroni every once in a while, the oath hasn't come up in a long time, until now. I'd almost forgotten it.

When we were shit-kicking kids on the Hill, we saw too many Steve McQueen movies where right and wrong glowed like neon signs even a blind man could see.

Right after we watched *The Great Escape* on Peggy's TV late one Friday night, Goat Johnson, always the romantic, said we ought to make some kind of pact, an oath, to always do the right thing, no matter how much trouble it caused us. So we invented the WWSD Oath: What Would Steve Do?

It was laughable, because we were pretty good at doing the wrong thing. What the oath seemed to mean to us, looking back on it, was that we'd never let the threat of a major ass-kicking keep us from defending our screwed-up version of honor and virtue.

The next day, we broke a Rolling Rock bottle out back of the Chuck Wagon. The ceremony involved blood and spit. Then Goat broke it into smaller pieces, and we each put one in our pocket—jagged, green and dangerous, a constant reminder.

I found mine a couple of years ago in the back of my sock drawer. I didn't throw it away, but I'm not carrying it in my pocket, either.

If one of us was skipping school and asked one of the others to skip with him, you did it, because he was your friend. If a bunch of kids from some other self-styled gang wanted to try to beat the crap out of us, we were at their service. It would be wrong to back down. If, when we got our licenses, we passed somebody on the road with the hood up, we stopped to help, even if the sight of three or four Hill boys climbing out of a beat-up jalopy usually scared the shit out of the stranded driver.

We've all broken quite a few oaths and screwed up in our various ways, but it's damn touching that Custalow remembers the oath and cares enough to remind me of it.

"Yeah," I say, as the sandwich continues its path to his mouth. "The oath. Right."

I don't feel like watching reruns, and I did promise Sarah Goodnight that I'd give her some guidance her first night on night cops. Custalow says reruns are fine with him.

I drop by the paper for an hour that turns into three. Sarah Goodnight needs to be officially introduced to whoever's at the precinct. When we get there, I'm glad to see Gillespie's red, shiny face, because I think I can count on him to keep an eye on her. He doesn't owe me any favors, but, Gillespie never knows when he's going to need one from me.

And then, against all odds, there is a dirt nap, down in Shockoe Bottom. Usually, those happen when all the bars close and the serious drunks spill out onto East Main. But this one happened at a little after ten, just as I was about to head down to Penny Lane and give the economy a shot in the arm.

She handled it like a pro. I tried not to hover, reminded not for the first time that she's only two or three years older than Andi. The age-inappropriate thing has never stopped me before, but when she asked me, on the way back to the paper, if I'd like to have a nightcap after she got off work, I surprised myself by begging off. Maybe I'm just getting old. Maybe it was the way she said "nightcap," like some little kid who'd picked up the phrase from an old black-and-white movie.

Maybe it was the goddamn oath.

CHAPTER THIRTEEN

Saturday

Job One today is finding Bump Freeman. Richard Slade wasn't quite sure which house is Freeman's present abode, and it isn't like I can pick up the damn phone and call Slade at the city lockup right now. So, off to the East End.

Nobody who lives there and doesn't know me is going to give me the time of day, which is nine thirty A.M. when I park the car out front and knock on Philomena Slade's front door.

It takes a little back-and-forth for her to decide that I might still be trying to help her son.

"So, are you on it or off it?" she asks me, with her arms crossed, standing like a bouncer behind her screen door.

"I've always been on it, Philomena."

"So who was that white boy you brought around here yesterday?"

I explain to her, as honestly as I can, about being taken off the story. She grills me awhile longer.

Then she sighs and finally opens the door.

"You're like one of those double agents," she says. "You playing both sides against the middle."

I want to tell her that I've been doing that my whole life, and making a pretty good living at it.

"Someday," she says, her hands on her hips, "you've got to pick one team or the other."

She tells me that Bump is living with his aunt, two blocks up the street on the other side. She gives me the house number.

"He wouldn't look me in the eye for twenty years after Richard went away," she says. "That boy has always been trouble. I think he was the one that got Richard and them to go to that white folks' swimming hole that night."

I thank her and start to leave.

"Wait a minute."

I turn, and she's putting on her overcoat.

"If they don't know you, they're not going to tell you anything."

I thank her. She gives me a hard stare.

"It isn't for you. It's for Richard."

The neighborhood goes downhill at a fairly steady pace between Philomena's place and our destination. Bump Freeman's aunt's house is in the middle of the block, better kept-up than most of the ones around it. A couple of them look like they're abandoned, waiting to be homesteaded by dealers or our fair city's growing homeless population.

The sight of a presumed white guy, even accompanied by one of the neighborhood's more solid citizens, apparently is enough to raise the alarm. A lady who appears to be about Philomena's age finally opens the door a crack and asks, none too friendly, "What you want?"

I start to talk, but then my guide steps up and does the heavy lifting for me, explaining that we just want to find out whether Bump can vouch for her son's comings and goings the week before, in the hours before Alicia Simpson's brains were splattered all over her nice new car.

"Bump hasn't done nothin.' He's been straight for almost two years," the woman starts to protest. Philomena says she knows that's true, but that Richard and Bump had a beer together down by the city docks, and it might help Richard if he could prove where he was.

"Bump didn't do nothin', " she says. "He just said he wanted to see Richard, talk to him, maybe be friends again."

Here, I step in, playing the moderately bad cop. I explain to Bump's aunt that I'm not a policeman, that I'm from the newspaper, and that I'm Richard Slade's cousin. She is on the verge of dismissing this as bullshit. She looks at Philomena, who nods her head.

"We intend to get to the bottom of this. I'm just trying to help Richard," I tell her. "And if you want to keep your nephew out of trouble, you'd be smart to help us. It'll be better if he tells me instead of having the cops come knocking, which they will pretty soon."

Actually, I can't believe the police haven't been here already.

She considers this and then goes down a long, narrow hallway that I presume leads to Bump Freeman's bed.

He comes out a few minutes later, rubbing his eyes, wearing pajama bottoms and a long-sleeved T-shirt. Assuming that he didn't come straight home from his shift, he's probably had only a few hours of sleep.

He nods at Philomena, who doesn't nod back, then looks at me.

"What you want?"

I tell him what everybody already knows, that Richard Slade is down in the city jail, accused of killing Alicia Simpson, and that he might be Richard's alibi.

"He didn't do nothing to that girl," Bump says as his aunt brings the cup of coffee that so far has not been offered to Philomena or me. I don't know whether he means back then or last week. Both Richard's mother and I have sense enough to let Bump talk.

I go through the whole chain of events, as told to us by Richard. They left for the docks at two, stopped by the convenience store about three thirty, back to Philomena's by four thirty. His story and Slade's are similar enough to be believable, considering that they almost certainly haven't talked in the last week—unless, of course, they plotted the whole thing out ahead of time.

"Well," I say, when he's done, "how do you know he 'didn't do nothing to that girl'?"

Bump stares at me, wondering if I'm making fun of him or not.

"He wouldn't," Bump finally says. "He was goin' on about how he had to forgive, for his peace of mind. He found Jesus or some such shit, when he was locked up. Me, I'd've cut the bitch up for bait . . ."

He stops and offers his apologies to his aunt and Philomena.

"And you didn't see him after four thirty?"

"No. I did call, though."

I'm thinking he tried to call later that day, like after the sun came up.

"When?"

He scratches and yawns.

"About half an hour later, I reckon."

"Like about five? Five a.m?"

He looks at me like I'm stupid.

"Yeah, A.M. The one in the morning."

"Why?"

"He left his cap in the car. I wanted to let him know."

"And he answered the phone?"

The look again.

"Yeah. But he sounded like he was about half asleep already. Said something about comin' by to pick it up sometime, but he never did."

"And you're pretty sure it was about five A.M."

"Yeah. It might of been five minutes one way or the other, but I remember lookin' at the clock when I came in, just a little after four thirty. I made myself a sandwich, and then I went to the bathroom, and then I called him."

I ask Bump for his phone number. He doesn't give it to me, but his aunt does.

I thank them both for their help.

"I ain't been much help to ol' Richard," he says, looking toward Philomena, who doesn't say anything.

We walk back. I ask Philomena if I can come inside for a minute, to check something.

I go to the phone and use the feature that shows who's called lately. Working back through several numbers I don't know, I finally come up with the one Bump Freeman's aunt just gave me. As it turns out, Bump's sense of time is pretty much dead on: 1/22/10. 5:01 A.M. 45 seconds.

I ask Philomena why Bump's call didn't wake her up. She tells me she unplugs the phone next to her bed before she goes to sleep. "Too many drunks and salesmen calling."

It isn't much. Slade and Bump Freeman could have cooked all this up. Bump probably would have been on board for a little revenge, even though it wasn't his ox being gored.

But Bump doesn't seem like what you would call clever. And if Bump isn't clever enough to be in cahoots with Richard Slade, then Slade was in his mother's house at one minute after five, fourteen minutes before Alicia Parker Simpson met her demise. Even if he had run out the door, jumped in somebody's car and driven like a bat out of hell, then slowed down just enough at that intersection to blow Alicia's brains out, I'm not sure he could have done it in fourteen minutes.

"Did that thing with the phone help?" Momma Phil asks me.

I told her that it certainly doesn't hurt.

I stop by the office. I seem to be putting in more hours working for free than I was when they were paying me.

There's one message, from Susan Winston-Jones.

"Call me," Bitsy says. "I just thought of something. About Alicia."

I go into one of the assistant editors' offices and shut the door. Bitsy answers on the third ring.

"Here's the thing," she says. "I've got this cellphone? But I don't use it that often. My kids nag me about it. They've got iPhones and Bluetooths, Blueteeth, whatever. All kinds of crap that I don't even know what they do. But I can't seem to get in the habit of even taking my damn cellphone with me. Or checking my messages."

Bitsy talks at a volume that indicates she doesn't really believe a phone can carry her voice all the way across town unless she speaks into it very loudly. I hold the phone a couple of inches from my ear and wait silently for the payoff.

"Well," she says, "I was going up to Fredericksburg yesterday, to see an old friend up there?—a friend of Alicia's, too, actually. We all grew up in the same neighborhood. We used to . . . but I digress."

Yes, I think, you do.

"So, for once, I thought to take the cellphone with me. And when I went to get it, where it had been charging for about ten days, for some reason I checked the calls missed.

"There were about a dozen, mostly from people who don't know what a cellphone idiot I am. But there was one that got my attention right away. Guess who it was from?"

"Alicia."

"How did you know that?"

"Lucky guess." Why else would you be calling me to tell me about it?

"Well," she says, "the phone said she called me on the nine-teenth, the Friday before she died. She sounded kind of, I don't know, weird, tired, something. Damn, why didn't she just call me on my regular phone? I always check my messages on that. She knows—she knew—what a Luddite I am."

I ask Bitsy what Alicia said, trying to head off another digression.

"She said she wanted me to know something, in case there was an emergency, in case something happened to her. She said she wasn't really that worried, but I could tell from her voice that she was. She said if she wasn't able to do it herself, that I should go to the bricks. I had to think for a minute, but then I knew."

I ask for the English translation. She said when she and Alicia were kids, they used to play this game. Their houses were just down the street from each other, and each one had a brick patio out back. The girls would leave messages for one another at a designated spot under loose bricks on each other's patio.

"I'd slip over there, after everyone went to bed, and leave her a note, or a little trinket, maybe a necklace or something. We eventually dug out little holes under the bricks. Then she'd go out when nobody was looking, move the bricks and retrieve it. Then, she'd do the same thing for me. We thought we were little spies. Nobody knew about the loose bricks except us. We couldn't have been more than ten or eleven, and we probably did it for a couple of years before we got too old for it."

"So," I say when Bitsy stops to take a breath, "she told you to go to the bricks."

"My parents are still alive, and they still live where I grew up," she says, now that she has her second wind. "I went over there this morning. They must have thought I was crazy, picking up those loose bricks and looking underneath them."

"And?"

"Nothing. Nothing but the little empty space we'd dug out underneath where she would leave my 'treasures,' she called them."

"So, dead end."

"Yeah. Dead end. But she was worried about something, Mr. Black."

"Willie."

"Willie. She was talking about it like she expected something to happen to her."

The Alicia Parker Simpson I remember, augmented with what I've heard, was quite capable of an overactive imagination, especially with the man she put behind bars for twenty-eight years recently released. But had Richard Slade made some kind of threat to her, maybe through an old acquaintance like Bump Freeman? I'm still trying to get my brain around the five A.M. phone call that Slade apparently took at his mother's house.

My head hurts.

I look up at the clock in the conference room. It's four thirty, and I'm long overdue for a smoke.

On the way to the elevator, I hear the opening bars of "Wooly Bully" and realize it's coming from my pants. I pull out my cellphone and stare at it in mute wonder when I hear Sarah giggling twenty feet away, holding her own phone to her ear.

I remember that she borrowed my phone briefly last night to call the office when I was giving her the Night Cops 101 course, just long enough to change the ringtone.

I answer, just so Sam the Sham and the Pharaohs will shut the fuck up.

Somebody, I tell Sarah, needs a spanking.

On the way outside, before I can change the ringtone, it rings again.

"Give it a rest, Sarah," I say before I'm interrupted.

"Willie," Jeanette says, "there's been an accident."

Andi was going down Main Street. Apparently she had the green light at Harrison, but the son of a bitch on Harrison apparently wasn't fazed by such trivial matters as stoplights. He T-boned her little Subaru on the driver's side, hard enough to drive it across two lanes and up on the sidewalk.

"Is she OK? Where is she?"

"They don't know," Jeanette says. "They took her to VCU."

It's a big teaching hospital. They don't take you there for hangnails.

When I arrive, it's the usual cluster-fuck trying to get information from the aggressively stupid people protecting the gravely ill from their loved ones. When I finally fight my way through security, Jeanette and Glenn are in a small waiting room reeking of anxiety and spent adrenaline. Everyone in here is waiting for news, and everyone knows there's no guarantee the news will be good.

Jeanette fills me in while Glenn, certainly the best of her two husbands, retreats into an inconspicuous corner.

They had a hard time getting in touch with Andi's next of kin, especially since Andi apparently didn't have her wallet or driver's license with her. The very phrase "next of kin" chills me. She was conscious enough to give them her name and address. They finally got one of her feckless roommates to answer the phone, but she didn't have any idea who Andi's parents were, or where, but she remembered that Andi had an old high school friend who worked at F.W. Sullivan's and—wonder of wonders—the friend was working that day and gave the authorities her own parents' number. And her parents, praise God, had Jeanette's number.

Andi has some kind of head injury, plus a broken left arm and some broken ribs. Jeanette hasn't seen her yet. By the time she got here, they'd already taken her to the operating room.

Hospital time is slow as molasses and faster than light. You sit there for what seems like hours, and you look up and see that ten minutes have passed. And then, in the twinkling of a derelict father's eye, three hours have disappeared.

It's sometime after eight fifteen when the surgeon comes in. We've already seen half a dozen life or death dramas played out in front us as we tried not to watch or hear. Sometimes you win, sometimes you lose. I'm just about to wet my pants as I realize the moment of truth is at hand.

The doctor, who might be thirty-five or fifty-five, gives nothing away. Life is cheap in his world, and I know he'll give it to us far more straight than we want it.

Andi, he says, is resting comfortably. She has been in and out of consciousness and has been given a lot of pain medication.

"Is she going to be OK?" I can't stop myself from asking.

The doctor doesn't answer for the three longest seconds of my life.

"We hope so," he says.

I note that we all goddamn hope so, that we were looking for something a little more definitive. Jeanette puts her hand lightly on my arm and I apologize.

The surgeon seems taken aback. I have a feeling that most people who spend time in this claustrophobic hell just accept what the doctor says and move on.

"She should get through this," he says after taking a deep breath. "She's young and healthy. But the next few days will tell."

Brain injuries, he goes on to tell us, sitting down now and really talking, are hard to diagnose and treat. Often, what's done is done, for better or worse.

"The fact that she is at least partially conscious is good news," he says, and then his beeper goes off, and he excuses himself, almost running out of the waiting area and down the long hallway. I realize he must do this all day, and I think that I'll never bitch about doctor's salaries again.

He's told us that we can see her, but only briefly. She's in intensive care, and we have to be buzzed in. There are supposed to be only two of us in her room at a time, so Glenn waits outside.

I'm not prepared for how beat up my daughter looks. I want to lie on top of her and somehow transfer all her pain to my worthless, dissipated body. Other than writing a few tuition checks, I've been a spectacularly negligent father, leaving her and her mother when they really needed me, for a woman whose charms had the shelf-life of your average dress shirt. Then, I was too wracked with guilt to force my way back into her life in any real way. Kate, Wife No. 3, was the one who finally got me to try, albeit too late, to rise above scum level as a father.

Andi's eyes are black. Her chest and the top of her head are bandaged, and her arm is hanging in a sling. She seems to be sleeping, but then she opens her eyes, which are more bloodshot than any I've ever seen.

"Hi, sweetie," Jeanette says, leaning down to kiss her gently on her cheek, just about the only place where it's possible to make contact with our daughter's flesh.

Andi mumbles something I can't hear. Then she looks over, and it seems that just moving her eyes brings her pain. She sees me and tries to give me a smile. It's then that I realize that at least two of her front teeth are missing.

I lose it. Jeanette puts her arm around me, and I finally man up as much as I can. Andi is looking at me, and she seems to want me to come closer.

I lean down over her and put my face as near to hers as I can.

"Don't worry, Daddy," she whispers, and then she drifts off to sleep again.

Nurses have been coming in about every ten minutes, and there seem to be about two for every patient in the ICU.

I kiss her cheek, too. The smell of Jeanette's perfume is still there. Then, I go outside and let Glenn take my place, the way he did all those years ago.

Glenn and Jeanette stay another twenty minutes while I wait outside, and then a nurse tells them it's time to leave, that Andi needs to rest.

I try to keep from wondering, as we all make our way down the zigs and zags that will finally release us to the world of good health, if I will ever see my daughter alive again.

It's already past ten o'clock. The nurse has convinced Jeanette, Glenn and me that there's nothing to be accomplished by staying longer. We agree to meet back at the hospital tomorrow morning.

I forget where I've parked my car, and by the time I finally find it, it's close to eleven o'clock. I feel empty in every way possible, driven nearly to panic at the thought that I might not have Andi forever. I am also empty on a more mundane level. I haven't eaten since noon. When my drive back to the Prestwould takes me within a block of Penny Lane, the car practically turns on its own.

Inside, I order a burger and some fries. And I start drinking.

I tend to drink for all kinds of reasons. To reward myself for taking a short ride on the wagon. To celebrate special events like birthdays, national holidays and sunsets. To be polite—nobody wants to be the only teetotaler at the party. There are plenty of good excuses to forget that once I start, it's hard to stop.

The worst, though, is the Feeling Sorry Drunk.

That's the one where you're so low, lower than Hell's basement, and you just want to wallow in it. The one where you've just seen the most important person in your world in close proximity to death, and you know how often you've failed her, and just about everybody else who counted on you, and you just want to climb up on the high board and do a swan dive into all the liquor there is.

Some people, in situations like this, pull it together and make some kind of vow to be better, set goals, turn a negative into a positive.

Or so I've heard.

I've had a late start and work hard to catch up. The Harps turn into bourbons on the rocks, because liquor is quicker. Before I know it, it's one thirty. I have a vague recollection of some co-workers coming in at some time. I only get up to step outside to smoke or to take a piss. I have a dim memory of an argument over the Super Bowl, of a broken glass, and an unfortunate incident with spectacularly bad aim in the men's bathroom.

If anybody but me realizes how fucked up I am, they don't give enough of a shit to do anything about it. Shortly after closing time, I'm in the Accord, on my eleven-block drive home, when I see this cop car coming right at me on the one-way street, blinding me with his blue light. I pull over, wondering what's so important that he's risked going the wrong way. As always when I'm blind drunk, I've been careful to go the speed limit, stay between the lines.

And then I see that other people are driving toward us, too. Everyone's going the wrong way but me.

Oops.

CHAPTER FOURTEEN

Sunday

A band of monkeys is playing the anvil chorus on my head. I look at the clock. Eleven thirty. Jesus, I haven't slept this late in years.

And then it starts coming back to me. I want to throw up.

Custalow comes in bearing coffee. He places it on the bedside table and leaves. On a better day, the sight of Abe tiptoeing his refrigerator-size frame out of the room would make me laugh, or at least smile.

I must have turned left on Franklin instead of Grace. Damn one-way streets. I didn't get more than three blocks, right by the public library, when they got me. It's hard to put it down to bad luck, since it was apparently my intention to drive all the way back to the Prestwould like that. Thank God it was two A.M. Not much traffic to scatter at that hour in downtown Richmond.

I wonder if they even bothered with the Breathalyzer, but then I do have some vague recollection of blowing into it. The cops were young, and they didn't have much patience with aging drunks. That's OK. I don't have much patience with myself right now.

It was Custalow who got me out of jail, I remember that. Must have been a few hours later, because I think I remember the sky getting light when we got back home. I was well on the way to sober by then.

Somehow in all that mess, Gillespie showed up, I guess down at the lockup. He's got reason enough to hate my ass, but I remember his asking me if I was OK, did I want him to call anybody. I gave him Custalow's number, and Abe got up from a perfectly good sleep to come down here and bail me out.

It's afternoon before I make my way down the hall. My legs feel like they weigh a thousand pounds. I think it's mostly the shame dragging me earthward. I would like very much to curl into a ball, turn out the lights and spend a few weeks in solitary. It is almost unendurable to think that it was a careless bastard like me who put my daughter's life in danger.

I thought I was past all this shit. When I was in my teens and twenties, I had a couple of DUIs. They cost me dearly, and I swore that wouldn't happen again, no matter how toasted I got. But you get stupid. And you pay the price.

"Want something to eat?" Custalow asks me. He's watching an old movie. I tell him not just yet, and he tells me Jeanette called. Shit. I remember that we were supposed to meet at the hospital at eleven. Andi. Fuck, fuck, fuck.

I ask him if he told Jeanette about last night, and he shakes his head.

"Just said you were a little under the weather."

I guess I'll have to tell her about it. But not right now.

I make a quick call to her cellphone. She says Andi's conscious but is sleeping a lot.

"You don't sound so good yourself," she says, and I hear in her voice the suspicion that it's not the twenty-four-hour virus keeping me down.

Don't worry, I tell her. It's not catching.

It takes me half an hour to get out the door. Custalow gets up and says he'll drive me. I tell him that I'm capable of driving myself, and he observes that I might be taking a chance, without a driver's license.

Oh, yeah. That, too.

"Just out of curiosity," I ask him as we're making our way to the elevator, "what did I blow? On the Breathalyzer."

He tells me, and I can't believe a man could nearly triple the state's definition of drunk in just three hours. I didn't feel that drunk, which I'm sure will carry a lot of weight in court. Maybe I can blubber about my poor, dear daughter at death's door and how distraught I was. If I do, I hope somebody shoots me. I wouldn't mind somebody doing that right now, anyhow.

"It could be worse," Custalow reminds me. "They don't send you to prison for DUI."

I thank him for the perspective. Right now, though, I need a lawyer.

I call Kate. She's at brunch with friends, apparently not including Mr. Ellis. I hear girls'-day-out shrieking in the background.

"Arrested? DUI? Oh, Willie."

Oh, Willie, my ass. There were plenty of times when either of us could have blown a point-two-oh when we were married and out partying. Somebody had to drive, and oftentimes it was the one who could actually fit the car key into the lock.

Still, I have to concede to myself that this might be a new low.

She says she'll look into it tomorrow morning, and find out how much it's going to cost me to get out of Stupid Town.

I thank her for her time.

I hang up before she can say "Oh, Willie" again.

Custalow drops me off at the hospital. I offer a half-assed excuse that Jeanette and Glenn seem to accept, probably because they're focused on Andi.

My daughter looks like holy hell, and she probably feels worse than she looks. Jeanette says she can't move around at all because of her ribs.

The good news, though, is that she is conscious. The nurses and other medical types come in every ten minutes or so to wake her up and make sure she's still among the living. Hell, I'm not complaining, although I'm sure Andi would if she were a little more coherent. I'm just glad to live in a town with a large, competent hospital.

While I'm there, they have what the doctors would call an incident. They have her open her eyes and follow the nurse's finger.

Except only the right eye follows. The left one is frozen. It freaks us out, but the nurse tells us that this is a common occurrence, and that it "usually" corrects itself. Still, they have one of the doctors on call in the ICU come look at her, and he says the same thing.

"Can't you fix it?" I ask him, knowing as I say it how stupid it sounds.

He indulges me, explaining in terms no liberal arts major can understand just what the problem is. We all nod our heads as if we know what the hell he's talking about.

A couple of hours later, Jeanette and Glenn go down to get some hospital cafeteria food, leaving me alone with Andi. She seems to be awake, so I start talking to her. She listens for a while, and then she says, "Daddy?" She says it as if she's just realized I was there.

I'm sitting in the big chair beside her bed, and she turns to look at me.

"Daddy," she says again, "where am I?"

That's a little disturbing, but I start explaining, as gently as possible, what's happened. Then I notice something. She's following me with both eyes. I want to yell, or cry, and she seems puzzled when I tell her what a good girl she is, as if she's six years old and learning to ride a bike.

I announce our good news to the nurses, as if I myself had somehow made my daughter's left eye work again. They smile indulgently, but when I ask the doctor if the "eye thing" is likely to happen again, he's noncommital.

Jeanette and Glenn are as happy as I was over the news that, for now, our daughter doesn't seem to have any problems that rest and luck can't fix. Glenn says prayer can't hurt either, but I'm thinking that he and my ex-wife have a better connection there than I do.

You have to go all the way to the parking lot to smoke. On the way, I pass two patients, pulling their IVs along with them, headed there, too. I'm sure that, if I were in dire enough straits to be treated in a major teaching hospital, I'd be able to quit smoking. Well, almost sure.

I check my phone messages. There's one from Baer, trying to pump me for information, insinuating that I owe him something, since my promised interview with Philomena Slade kind of fell apart.

It occurs to me, halfway through the second coffin nail, that there may be a way for the tireless Mr. Baer to help me while he thinks I'm helping him.

I go back to Andi's room and stay for another hour. Jeanette says she's going to stay longer, which probably means until they toss her out. Glenn's going home to make sure their sons haven't burned down the house. I leave with him, telling Jeanette I'll try to come by later. She smiles, fully aware of how seldom I actually do something when I say I'm going to "try."

I do tell her, on the way out, about last night.

She puts her hand on top of mine.

"Oh, Willie," she says.

I could have called Custalow back for a ride, but the paper's only a few blocks from the hospital. As I walk in the front door, I can look down Franklin and see where Richmond's finest found fault with my driving last night.

Baer's in the office. He doesn't seem to have much of a life outside the newspaper. I don't think he and Sarah Goodnight are "seeing" each other anymore. I have to admit that, self-serving backstabber that he is, he does work.

I ask Baer what he's up to, and he says "Richard Slade."

I note that the whole sorry Slade-Simpson story appears to have been put to sleep by powers above us.

"I dunno," Baer says, and frowns. "Something doesn't seem right."

Really.

"Like what?"

He scratches his head.

"Like the way Alicia Simpson's sister wants us to stop writing about it. Like how Richard Slade spent twenty-eight years in prison for something he didn't do and never got written up for one single violent act—not even a fistfight—and then he murders Alicia the first week he's out."

"Maybe he'd been saving it up, for twenty-eight years."

Baer looks at me.

"No, it doesn't make sense."

Baer's getting warm. It's probably time to give him a little information. If nothing else, it'll be a small payback for the fact that I couldn't get Philomena to talk to him.

So, I tell him about the five A.M. call.

"And it was recorded there, on the incoming calls ID list, at his mother's house?"

I nod.

"Damn. Why didn't you tell me before?"

I tell him that I just found out about it yesterday morning. Plus, we're not even supposed to be pursuing this end of the story anymore.

"But we are," Baer says. "Or at least you are."

I tell him I've got lots of free time these days.

Sarah comes over to us, yawning as if she hasn't been awake all that long. Something about the way she greets him and the almost-bashful smile with which he responds makes me wonder if she hasn't had a relapse and again hooked up with Mr. Baer. Well, she's done worse. At least he's age-appropriate.

Baer tells her we're talking about the Richard Slade case, as if we're cops instead of just reporters meddling where we probably shouldn't be.

Sarah has no intention of leaving, so I figure she might as well hear it, too.

"I could use some help," I tell Baer and Sarah. The way Baer's eyes shine makes me wish I'd kept my own counsel. He'll be on this like a beagle on bacon.

But I've long since used up all the good will I might ever have had when it comes to Lewis Witt, and it would be nice if someone could still go over there and get a foot inside the door long enough to make Lewis aware of that phone call and its possible implications. Plus, I'm not even getting paid to do this crap.

"Shouldn't you just call the cops?" Sarah asks.

I tell her that I'm going to do that, but not just yet.

"You want to do it yourself," she says, laughing and pointing a finger.

No, I tell her and Baer. I'm not even on the story anymore, just trying to help out. I don't even know why, but I tell them about the family connection.

"He's your cousin," Baer says. "Damn."

I'm not sure Baer was totally aware of my ethnic heritage until now. He's reasonably color-blind, and it probably never occurred to him to wonder where I got my great tan.

"So you probably shouldn't have been on this story anyhow."

I tell him that if anyone farther up the food chain ever hears about this, I'll have his ass.

"Well," Sarah says, "mum's the word, then. We certainly wouldn't want you to have our asses."

Baer laughs, a little too heartily for my liking, but he takes the vow of silence.

What I need, I tell him, or them, is for someone to get the word to Lewis that there is evidence of a five A.M. call to Richard Slade, and a guy who'll say he talked to Slade at that time, on Slade's home phone.

Time to do a little cage-rattling.

"I can do that," Sarah says. "I can go by there this afternoon, see if she'll let me in."

Baer says he should be the one to go over there, but Sarah correctly reminds him that he might be wearing out his welcome as well, having appeared there before with the notorious Willie Black in tow.

So now there are three of us, kind of like the Mod Squad— one white, one blonde, one about one-half black—although neither of my dewy-eyed co-conspirators would be old enough to understand the allusion.

I walk over to see Les and Peggy. I ask Les if he wants to go for a walk, and he says yes. Peggy bundles him up against the chill, after he tries to leave the house with just a jacket. As Les becomes more childlike, Peggy becomes motherly. Hell, I don't remember her taking that much care with me, her only begotten son. But I'm still here, so I guess she did something right.

"Don't let him stay out too long," she admonishes me.

The house farther down Laurel where I almost burned to death fifteen months ago is still sitting there, its black eyes staring out at the empty winter street, still waiting for some demolition firm to put it out of its misery.

We walk down to the overlook and watch the James rush past below us.

"It's cold," Les says, as if it's just occurred to him. "How long till baseball season?"

I tell him "too long," and we head back.

Awesome Dude has returned from his daily perambulations. Even though he has the option of a roof over his head, what Peggy calls "homeless insurance," he is not a creature to sit by the fire. All those years of rambling have made the sedentary life foreign to him.

We tell him and Peggy about walking by the ruins of the late David Shiflett's home.

"Dude," Awesome says, "that place scares me. I walk a block over just so I don't have to see it."

He and Peggy have shared the better part of a joint, and soon the two of them and Les are more or less transfixed by an old William Powell movie. Peggy and Awesome ascribe more humor to it than it deserves. Les and I exchange a glance. He smiles and shakes his head.

Les has been the adult, caring for Peggy better than any of her three husbands or assorted and sordid other boyfriends did. Now, with dementia scooping out bits of his brain with a melon baller, the dynamics are shifting. Peggy, Les or even the late-arriving Mr. Dude takes the adult supervision role, according to who is the most sane and/or sober at the time.

I fill Peggy in on what's happening with Richard Slade.

"Philomena must be going nuts," she says. "But you make it sound like maybe he didn't do it."

"I don't know that. We're trying to find out."

"Well," she says, turning back to the TV as an ambulance-chasing commercial, urging everyone who's short of breath to get a lawyer, fades out, "you be careful."

"You know," she says, taking another toke as William Powell reemerges to steal her attention, "I think I might have that mesothelioma."

No doubt, I assure her.

I let myself out, wondering if Sarah's having any luck storming the fortress that is Lewis Witt.

Back at the Prestwould, Custalow's glued to the boob tube, too, but at least he's multitasking, munching away on some take-out pizza. He once told me he was incapable of boredom, and I believe him. He doesn't seem to have any real hobbies, hasn't even hooked up with a girlfriend that I know of since he traded his park bench for my guest bedroom.

He asks me about Peggy and Les. He stops by and sees them from time to time when he makes a trip into our old neighborhood.

The phone rings half an hour after I get home.

It's Sarah.

"I was going to call you," I tell her.

She talks over me.

"Wesley Simpson is missing."

Sarah says she rang the doorbell three times before a man who turned out to be Carl Witt answered it.

"I told him who I was, and that I was from the paper, and he kind of blanched. He said that they didn't have anything to say, that they were kind of having an emergency. I could hear somebody on the phone in the next room, and I figured it must be Lewis."

He was starting to close the door on her when she played the only card she had.

"He didn't really seem that pissed," Sarah says. "He just seemed kind of, you know, bedraggled, like he'd maybe been up all night.

"But when I told him about the phone call, and told him we had a witness who said he'd called Slade and talked to him at five A.M., he stopped. And I heard the other person, Lewis, put the phone down. And it got kind of quiet."

"Did they throw you out?"

"Not right then. Lewis came to the door. I recognized her from pictures I'd seen in the paper. She asked me to repeat what I'd just said, about the phone call, and then she said it was bullshit, that they were just trying to make a few headlines, and that she was going to call some guy named Whitehall, something like that, right then."

"Giles Whitehurst?"

"Yeah, I think so."

I tell her who Giles Whitehurst is.

"Am I going to get fired, Willie?"

I assure her she isn't and hope I'm right.

"She mentioned your name, too. She said she bet she knew who put me up to this. 'That damn Willie Black.' I told her I'd come on my own, but I don't think she believed me.

"Then she started ragging on me for disturbing them 'in their time of grief.' She must have been a little unhinged, because she starts talking to her husband about it, with me standing right there.

"She said she'd called the police, but that they were, quote, 'too damn lazy' to go find a man who obviously was off his medication."

"Did she mention Wesley by name? I mean, how did you know she was talking about her brother?"

"Oh, yeah. When I was leaving, just before they did shut the door in my face, she started kind of yelling at her husband, or the world, or something. She said, 'Wesley, you idiot. Why now? Why now?' And that was the last I heard before the door slammed."

I tell her she did a good job.

Like Lewis Witt, I'm wondering why Wes Simpson has chosen this particular moment to go off his meds.

CHAPTER FIFTEEN

Monday

I get the story from that fount of knowledge, Susan Winston-Jones.

I hear her voice on the answering machine and pick up.

"Hey," Bitsy says. "I thought I'd give you a call, in case your keen reporter's instinct hasn't picked up on this tidbit already."

She sounds as if she might be mocking me. I guess correctly that she's talking about Wesley Simpson.

I tell Bitsy that I didn't know he was still hearing those voices telling him to stop taking his meds and go nuts.

"I think you stop taking your meds and then you hear the voices," Bitsy says, "but at least he didn't stay gone long this time."

"They've got him already?"

"Yeah. Lewis must have raised holy hell at some level way higher than Richmond's finest."

They found him in Arkansas. He was, for reasons that we'll never know, I guess, in some town in the northeast corner of the state, Blytheville. Between the time he rented a car at the Memphis airport and the time he tried to pay for his room at a Holiday Inn, Lewis had managed to have his credit card canceled. When he made a fuss about it, they called the local cops, who found out they had a missing person, presumed dangerous, on their hands.

"Anyhow," Bitsy says, "I think Carl was flying out to Memphis today to get him and bring him back. He's lucky they didn't keep him in jail. I understand he hit a cop."

Money talks, I remind her. Then I ask her how she found all this out so quickly. I figured she'd know something about it, but not this much.

"Oh," she says, laughing, "I have my ways. Carl Witt and my brother were in the same fraternity at U.Va. Carl called him last night and asked him to meet him for a drink or three. Carl kind of likes to drink, I think, and I imagine he felt like he needed to get away from Lewis's ranting for a while."

So, sometime after Sarah Goodnight was shown the door at close range yesterday, Lewis must have gotten the call from Arkansas.

"Fast work," I say.

"Better than the last time. This time, they found the car."

I have to ask.

"Why are you telling me all this?"

She's uncustomarily quiet for a few seconds.

"I don't like this," she says at last. "I don't like what happened to my friend, and I don't think I like what's happening to that man they arrested for it."

Fair enough, I say. I'm not exactly sold on the police version of things either.

"I figure," she goes on, "if I can shed a little sunlight on what's happening, maybe somebody will find the truth, just lying there like a diamond amid all the broken glass."

I tell her that's very poetic, and then I sincerely thank her. I tell her that I'm not allowed to write about the case right now, or even to work at the newspaper, but that I'm passing my information to somebody who can help her shine truth's own flashlight on this mess.

"You mean that girl who went to Lewis and Carl's yesterday?"

"You do get around," I say.

"Like I said, I have my sources."

"Stay in touch," I tell her, and she hangs up.

The sun is streaming in the east-facing windows. Not being able to legally drive is going to be a big problem, I can tell. It's a good thing I live within walking distance of the newspaper (assuming I get to work there again) and right on the bus line. The hospital, where I'm eventually headed, would be a haul otherwise, and Custalow doesn't have time to be my full-time personal chauffeur.

I've arranged for Kate to meet me for coffee at Perlie's first, though, so I can probably forgo the services of our fine transit system this morning if I don't piss my ex-wife off too much.

When she walks in, I can see she looks a little tired. She's talking on her cellphone, as usual, as she slides into the booth, facing me. She nods slightly and holds up a finger.

"Sorry," she says when she momentarily returns from cell-world to the one where people have face-to-face conversations. "It was Marcus. He wants us to meet with Slade today. I don't know, Willie. It's not looking good. But let's talk about you. You really ought to drink less, or at home, or something."

I concede that this is true. Protest is futile. As one of my former wives, she knows too well what alcohol, nicotine and Mr. Johnson, a.k.a Willie's willie, have done to the general well-being of myself and those I profess to love.

We order omelets, hash browns and coffee. As we're eating, she lays out my future. She thinks that the system won't be overly harsh with me, but that I'm likely to be restricted to work-only driving for six months or so, in addition to making a hefty withdrawal from my not-so-hefty checking account.

"And your insurance company is going to drop you," she adds.

"I hope I can still afford to pay the rent," I say.

She doesn't smile and says she hopes so, too.

She pats her mouth with her napkin, wiping a bit of egg that was stuck on her upper lip.

"You know," she says, "you might want to think about AA."

"Isn't that for alcoholics?"

She gives me the thinnest smile imaginable.

She gives no indication that last Wednesday's little afternoon delight was anything but an immediately regretted lapse in judgment and good sense. She gives her watch a surreptitious glance.

"I might have something that would make Mr. Slade's day a little brighter," I tell her, and Kate is suddenly all ears.

I hadn't exactly planned to tell her, and maybe I'm telling her now just to keep her in my sight for a few more minutes, impress her with my reporterly skills.

I tell her about Bump Freeman and the phone call.

"Why the hell didn't Slade tell us about it?" she asks.

"I don't know. Freeman said he sounded like he was half asleep. He never came by the next day like he said he would."

"Well, by the end of the next day, he was already in jail."

Kate suggests that perhaps, as I have nothing else to do, I might accompany her over to the jail, where she's supposed to meet Marcus Green. I check my watch and figure I can spare a couple of hours.

"Oh, yeah," I tell her as she's pulling away from the curb, "Wesley Simpson went missing. They found him somewhere in Arkansas."

She stops, halfway out in traffic, finally moving on when the guy behind her sits on his horn. She looks at me and shakes her head.

"Any more surprises? He seemed a little spooky to me, at the funeral. Didn't Clara say he'd done that before?"

"Yeah, but the timing's kind of strange, and Sarah said Lewis seemed pretty upset about it."

"Well, he is her brother. She's running out of sibs. Who's Sarah?"

I explain about Sarah volunteering to go to the Witts' front door, since I was on Lewis's shoot-to-kill list and not getting paid by the newspaper at present.

"You always were good at getting the girls to do favors," she says.

"You're smirking."

"Wait, let me guess. She's about twenty-three, blonde, pretty, looking for a mentor?"

"Wrong. She's twenty-four."

"Oh, Willie," she says, using much the same tone as she did when she found out about my little DUI adventure yesterday.

At the jail, Marcus is waiting for us. Kate brings him up to speed on the five A.M. call. Marcus stares for a second. Then he smacks his bald, shiny head.

"He didn't say a damn thing to me about that."

Inside, I'm allowed to accompany Richard Slade's crack defense team to the interview room.

Marcus cuts to the chase.

"What about that phone call Bump Freeman gave you? Were you going to tell us about that? Do you want to spend the rest of your life in prison, or worse?"

Slade looks genuinely confused.

"Five A.M. About the same time you were allegedly murdering Alicia Parker Simpson."

"I—I don't remember nothin' like that. I mean, why wouldn't I tell you if I remembered it?"

Something occurs to me. It's a long shot, but that's all we have.

"Richard," I interrupt, "were you taking any kind of medication, like sleeping pills or something?"

He thinks for a few seconds.

"I couldn't sleep," he says finally. "I was kind of jazzed up, after talking to Bump and all. I guess it's just being somewhere without bars, with cars and crickets and all. I'd mentioned it to Momma the night before, and she gave me some of her pills."

"Do you know what it was?"

"I don't know. Never heard of it. A-something. Amber. Amway. Something like that . . ."

"Ambien?" Kate asks.

"Yeah, that's it! Ambien. I took one after I got back to the house."

Kate and I exchange glances.

"What?" Marcus Green asks.

Sometime in our first two years of marriage, Kate had a bout of insomnia, and her doctor prescribed Ambien.

One night, she'd fallen asleep before me. Sometime after one, the phone rang, and I answered it. It was Kate's mother, and it was serious. It's always serious that time of night. Kate's father was having chest pains. She was calling from the emergency room. Kate must have talked with her for five minutes, and then hung up. She told me her father was stable, and that there wasn't any reason to rush to the hospital. I should've made her go right then, but I didn't. Five minutes later, Kate was asleep again.

When I woke up at seven to take a piss, I thought I'd better wake Kate, too. I was sure she'd want to get over to the hospital right away.

I had to shake her a couple of times before she opened her eyes.

"Shouldn't you get up, sweetie?" I asked. "Your mom's probably waiting for you."

"What?"

"At the hospital."

"Hospital?"

She didn't remember a damn thing. She was mortified that she hadn't rushed right over when she got the call she didn't remember getting, and she never took Ambien again.

Kate explains that it is possible to do things under the influence of some of our finer sleep-inducing drugs and then not remember them later.

"So," Richard Slade says, not quite seeming to believe it, "I could have talked to Bump and not even remembered it?"

Kate tells him that's so.

"Damn."

Of course, I'm wondering what else you could do under the influence of Ambien and not remember, but keep it to myself.

We talk a bit more, and then the three of us leave.

"In the future," Marcus tells me, "you might want to keep us informed on shit like this."

"When I'm working for you," I tell him, "I might do that."

I get a call from Sarah while Kate's driving me to the paper.

"You might want to be here for this," she says. "Wheelie's about to fire Mark."

"He's going to can Baer?"

As much as I have grown to dislike the guy who seems to be permanently affixed to my coattails, this doesn't seem right. Baer's sucked up enough to Wheelie, Grubby and anybody else in a suit to be fireproof. Or so I thought.

"Why?"

"Oh, he put something on his blog about Wesley Simpson going missing. It wasn't much, just a couple of paragraphs."

I guess that somewhere deep inside Baer's upwardly mobile DNA a few strands of journalist exist. He couldn't resist the urge to print—or at least commit to the ether—the truth.

"I tried to stop him," Sarah says, and I'm depressed by how upset she sounds. Not that it's any of my business. Right.

I ask Kate to drop me by the paper.

"More news to hoard?" she says.

"Nothing new. It's just that half the town probably knows about Wes Simpson by now."

"I hope this doesn't get your little mentee in trouble."

She's definitely smirking now.

"Just because you imagine it," I say, "doesn't mean it's so."

We're at the paper. I get out of the car. I should just keep walking, but I walk around to her side and ask what I think is a pertinent question:

"Besides, what's it to you?"

The sparsely populated newsroom is quiet. A couple of the features reporters look kind of lonely.

"They're up in Grubby's office," Sarah tells me when I reach her desk.

Upstairs, Sandy McCool is her usual poker-faced self. When she informs me that Grubby's in a meeting, I tell her I know, that I'm there for the meeting, too.

"I don't think so," she says.

I like Sandy. She's a pro. But when I realize that I'm three steps closer to Grubby's office than she is, and when I further deduce that it's unlikely Grubby has locked his door, I spring into action, spring being a relative word. At any rate, I'm able to beat Sandy to the publisher's Holy of Holies and step in unannounced and very definitely uninvited. I'm only slightly winded.

Baer is there, with Wheelie sitting beside him. Our managing editor looks decidedly uncomfortable. He'll probably be splattered with some of the blame for the unfortunate blog that no doubt has already elicited a call from Giles Whitehurst or perhaps Lewis Witt herself. Baer looks nervous. This won't look good on his résumé. It's much easier to get a job at the *Post* if you haven't just been fired.

James H. Grubbs, who sits facing them, picks up the phone as if to call security. He holds the receiver a foot or so in the air, then sets it down.

"Willie," he says. "I should have known you had a hand in this. Do you really want to make that suspension permanent?"

I assure Grubby that this is not my fondest wish, but that there is more to the story than even the doughty Mr. Baer knows.

"I don't really care how much of the story there is," Grubby says. "The story does not exist. Until Richard Slade's trial, there is no story. Period."

"Maybe you don't care, then, that Wesley Simpson's already been found and is, as we speak, headed back to Richmond."

"I know that," Grubby says, confirming what I already pretty much knew: Either our board chairman or Lewis Witt has been lighting his ass up already.

Might as well take a chance.

"There are a few things that you probably don't know."

Grubby is silent.

"When we found out Wesley Simpson was missing, I knew that I wasn't allowed to put anything on my blog, so I convinced Baer to let me put it on his."

Baer looks like he wants to refute this for a half-second, not enough time for either of my bosses to notice. Then Baer, quick learner that he is, closes his mouth.

"He didn't know how much of a shitstorm this would kick up," I add. "I just told him we wanted to see if we could ferret out the truth."

"The truth," Grubby says, as if it's an obscenity. "The truth is, I'll give you a one-minute head start before security comes and has you arrested for trespassing in my office."

"But, Grubby," I continue, already off the high board now and hoping there's water in the pool, "you need to know a couple of other things."

I lay out what I know so far: How we have a witness who will swear he talked to Richard Slade on his home phone around five A.M., just before Alicia Simpson was murdered, and proof that the call was made. How an unnamed source says Alicia was writing a manuscript at the time of her death and was fearful that something was going to happen to her. How I am close to laying my hands on that manuscript. (OK, I'm stretching the truth a little there.) I also mention that a man who never harmed a soul in twenty-eight years behind bars didn't seem like a likely candidate for first-degree murder.

"Do you realize how stupid we'll all look if we don't follow this thing through, and then the Innocence Project comes in and gets his ass off a second time? The paper—hell, the whole damn city will look like assholes."

I know I'm drawing to an inside straight here, but I don't have much to lose.

Grubby is quiet. I'm standing, kind of wedged in a corner. Wheelie and Baer are afraid to look up.

"OK," he says at last. "You have a week. I'll tell . . . whoever I have to tell that it was your mischief that caused this, and that you're fired. That shouldn't be too hard a story to sell. And, if at the end of a week you haven't produced the goods, you really are fired, plain and simple."

"And if I come through?"

"Then," Grubby says, "you'll have to trust me to make the suits happy."

Trusting Grubby may not be the smartest move, but what are my choices?

I walk the few blocks to the hospital. Outweighing all the crap that's been coming down lately, Andi seems to have turned some kind of corner and appears to be beyond the danger zone. She's being moved to the step-down unit, and they might release her in a day or so, but she's going to need to have a lot of rehab.

"Is she really that close to being released?" I ask a nurse, a tall African-American woman who looks as if she doesn't have much time for civilians' dumb questions.

"If she wasn't," she says, only slowing down enough to let me walk with her for a few yards, "they wouldn't release her."

Still, part of me thinks they just need her damn bed, or her health insurance only covers five days.

I talk with Andi for a few minutes and then she says she's tired and drifts off. It goes like that for a couple of hours. When she's asleep, I brush her blonde hair, crushed and dirty, with my hands and close my eyes. I don't pray for things these days; it would just be hypocritical and ridiculous. It seems OK, though, to say 'Thank you,' in case Anybody's there.

I'm dying for a cigarette. When Jeanette and Glenn come back from grabbing a late lunch, I tell them that I'll be back later, or maybe tomorrow.

"She's going to need some rehab," Jeanette tells me. "They're not sure she's ever going to have full use of that left arm."

At least, I think, she's right-handed.

"What can I do to help?"

I know as I'm saying it that it sounds like bullshit. People always ask what they can do, and I know that real friends, real family, will offer to do specific things, insist on doing them, really.

Jeanette, though, instead of waving off my feeble offer, says, "Well, she might need a place to stay for a few weeks."

I nod my head.

"The boys have their room, and now that Glenn's mother is living with us . . . well, we just have the three bedrooms."

I nod again. I'd forgotten that she and Glenn, good souls that they are, had taken in his mother for what probably will be her last days, weeks, months or years.

And I do have room. No denying that. The space Custalow and I occupy is larger than Jeanette and Glenn's house.

The idea of Andi living with me pleases and terrifies me.

"You know I can't drive right now."

"Well," Jeanette says, "if it's going to be too much trouble . . ."

"No. No. It's just . . . Let me see what I can do."

The look Jeanette gives me pretty much says it all.

"Well," she says, "I'm sure we can work something out. Don't worry."

I assure her that I can figure "something" out. She tells me again it's OK, the way she used to after we split up, when I would have some lame-ass excuse to miss one of Andi's soccer games or piano recitals.

I make my way out, saying hasty goodbyes to my ex-wife and her husband.

There is no one in the world who means more to me than Andi, I think to myself as I'm sucking down my second cigarette waiting in the cold for the city bus. If I wasn't in the middle of all this mess with Richard Slade, if I had my driver's license, if we didn't live all the way up on the sixth floor—I mean, what if she had some kind of seizure or something?

I am a gold medalist in talking myself out of doing the right thing.

CHAPTER SIXTEEN

Tuesday

The short walk over to Laurel Street takes less than fifteen minutes, but it's cold enough to freeze the balls off a brass monkey. I stop off at the 821 for some coffee on the way and run into Awesome Dude. He's wearing what looks like Les's parka, which probably weighs about as much as he does and pretty much swallows him. Awesome hasn't gained an ounce, I don't think, since the first time I saw him more than twenty-five years ago. Maybe I can make my next (and first) million writing a diet book. The Homeless Diet: How sleeping outdoors, eating in soup kitchens and drinking at least thirty-two ounces of cheap red wine a day can help you keep your youthful figure, if not your teeth.

Strangely, not even living mostly indoors at Peggy's, sleeping in a reasonably soft bed in the English basement and eating two or three times a day has changed that.

"Dude!" he says.

"What brings you out today?"

"I might ast you the same thing," he grins, showing off his lovely gums, interspersed with the odd tooth.

Awesome still likes the street, even on a day like this, although he doesn't turn down a roof over his head, either. But somehow he has enough change to pay for his own cup of coffee, and here he is.

He waits for me to order mine, black with lots of sugar, and we walk back toward Peggy's.

Peggy and Les are at the table. Peggy's eating cold cereal and Les is having a banana with his coffee. I wonder if Peggy has stopped cooking breakfast. She's never been a great cook, anyhow. Awesome opens the refrigerator door and takes out some bacon and a couple of eggs. He's the only one in my mother's little lunatic asylum who seems interested in a hot meal.

Peggy doesn't seem to have had her first toke of the day yet, and she asks me to fill her in on Andi's condition. I mention that I might have to take her to my place for a while.

"Oh," Peggy says, "she can stay here with us."

I suddenly realize that being under the care of Abe Custalow and me isn't the worst thing that could happen to my daughter.

"And you," she says. "Are you out of a job for good, or just temporarily?"

I tell her I'm working on it.

"You got fired?" Les asks. Every day is a new day with Les, full of surprises after the dementia fairy comes to his bed at night and erases the previous day from his mind, or large parts of it at least. Sometimes, it doesn't seem so bad being Les.

"What about that boy?" Peggy asks. "Philomena's son."

"We're working on that," I tell her.

"I wouldn't mind seeing Philomena again sometime. I liked her."

I mention that this might be possible.

On the way back to the Prestwould, I hear a car coming up behind me. It slows to a crawl. I look over, and there's R. P. McGonnigal, friend o' my youth.

"Hey," he says. "Where've you been?"

Nowhere much, I tell him. I have missed a couple of poker nights, but I tell him that I'll definitely be at the one next week, having nothing else to do.

We catch up. R.P. has a new boyfriend. This one drives a city bus. Images of Ralph Kramden flash before me. R.P., something of gentle soul himself, likes them a little on the rough side.

"What happened to the butcher?" I ask, and kind of wish I hadn't. R.P. looks a little sad, and I know that his affairs of the heart are just as serious as mine, maybe more so.

"Just didn't work out. We still talk, but . . . it's just not working. You know."

After three marriages, yes, I know.

R.P. has to be at the office in twenty minutes. We promise to have a beer together, and definitely I'm on for poker next week. I promise to bring Custalow, too. It's about the only time Abe and I see R.P. and Andy Peroni, the two members of our old wrecking crew still in town and alive. It's crazy. We live blocks apart and can go months without seeing each other.

My cellphone interrupts a peaceful if chilly walk back home.

The voice on the other end is familiarly breathless.

"Willie? It's Bitsy."

Susan Winston-Jones sounds like she's in the middle of a hurricane.

"Oh," she says. "That was just the vacuum. I'm multitasking."

"Is this a social call?"

I hear her snort.

"Good one. No, it's not a social call. I have some very important information."

"Hit me."

"Well," she says, "for one thing, Wes is back home. They got him back last night. He's over at Lewis and Carl's now, I think. That's what I heard this morning, anyhow."

"You ought to be a reporter, with your contacts."

"What's it pay?"

"Not enough."

Her well-connected source has told her that Wes Simpson had to be transported back to Richmond in restraints—"like a straitjacket or something"—and that if somebody hadn't pulled some very expensive strings, he'd still be in Arkansas, probably in some nuthouse.

"Well," I say, "he's lost it before."

"I don't know, Willie. Something isn't right. I mean, Alicia and Wes were always close. She worried about him all the time, what was going to happen to him. But something's happened, something above and beyond Wes's usual schizophrenic disasters. I can just feel it."

"I wish I could talk to him."

Bitsy laughs.

"Fat chance of that."

I tell Bitsy I have to be somewhere in half an hour.

"Where? The unemployment office? Wait, wait. That was cruel. I'm sorry. But there was something else I had to tell you."

"I'm still here."

"Well, you know the thing about 'going to the bricks'? I don't know what I was thinking about, but last night it came to me. It wasn't my bricks. It was her bricks."

I tell Bitsy I need just a tad more clarity.

She sighs, impatiently I think.

"The bricks, where we used to leave each other little gifts? Remember?"

"Yeah, I remember."

"Well, what if she meant that whatever she'd hidden, she'd hidden under the bricks at her place? What if she left something out there at her parents' old place? I mean, it's possible, right?"

Yes, I concede that it is possible. Whether it's probable or not is another question. Maybe Alicia Simpson left something under the bricks in the patio at her parents' old home. Maybe it was something meaningful. Maybe I'll wake up tomorrow morning with a full head of hair.

"So," I say, "are you going over there to check it out?"

"I can't. Not for a few days."

The Winston-Jones family, it turns out, is getting ready to leave for a little skiing vacation. They won't be back until the weekend.

There's another reason, too.

"I really feel uneasy," she says, "snooping around over there. Some of this has got me spooked a little."

So, I ask what should be done. I know the answer already.

"Well," she says, drawing the word out as if she's just come up with a brand-new solution, something she never thought of before, "you could maybe go over there? And check it out?"

"I think that's called trespassing."

"Only if you get caught."

I note that I am on the cusp of joblessness and losing my driver's license for an extended period of time. The count is no balls and two strikes, and I need to foul a couple off, work the pitcher a little. I do not at present need to go down swinging.

"Well," Bitsy says, "you do what you have to do. I was just passing along some information, hoping some intrepid reporter would jump all over it."

She sounds smug. She knows she has me. She probably knows I won't farm this one out, either. I can't send Sarah Goodnight out there snooping around with a garden spade and penlight in the middle of the night, and I don't want Baer horning in any more than I've let him already.

Dammit, I want this one myself.

"I'll call you when I get back," Bitsy says.

"Break a leg," I tell her.

"You're supposed to say that before a play, not a ski trip. . . . Oh, I get it. Funny."

I need to see the Quarry again, and those houses above it. I think they call it casing the joint. I call Kate.

"The Quarry? What for?"

I don't tell her everything, as was my custom even when we were married. I tell her that there's something I want to check out there, and I'll tell her if I see what I think I'm going to see.

I hear her sigh.

"Shithead," she says. "Why should I take off from work to chauffeur a wild goose chase?"

"Because it might be what you and Marcus need to get Slade out of jail. Besides, you're on sabbatical."

She's quiet for a few seconds, then tells me that she can't get away until after one. She'll pick me up in front of the Prestwould.

I've been outside ten minutes, standing in the slush, when she pulls into the handicap space.

She motions with her hand as I start to get in, and I take one last puff before throwing the cigarette to the curb and stomping it out.

"You're going to make the whole car smell like tobacco," she says. "You know, when that shit finally kills you, they won't even be able to give your clothes to Goodwill. Your car's going to be a total loss, too."

And yet, I'm thinking, you were able to hold your breath long enough to do the nasty with me last week.

Tired of lecturing, she looks over at me, shakes her head, and asks, "Where to?"

The Quarry is just as abandoned as you might think it would be on the first of February. Not a soul in sight. I'm not planning to stay here for more than a minute or two, then check out the houses up above.

Kate parks the car. I walk over to the padlocked gate, and it looks like somebody's broken the lock.

"Somebody must have been dying for a January swim," Kate says.

I can't think of a better explanation. There's nothing worth stealing in here.

There's still a little bit of snow that hasn't melted, here in the shadows. I can see the footprints. I follow them to the dressing rooms, to the men's side. Kate's right behind me. She's probably as well off with me as back at the car. Plus, I can see that the prints go both in and out.

The electricity's been turned off for the winter, apparently, and I have to leave the door wide open to see anything. When my eyes adjust, I see the photograph, framed and sitting there on the bench.

Kate looks at it, and we look at each other.

"What's that supposed to mean?" she asks.

I have a hunch, but I'm not saying anything right now.

"No telling."

"No telling as in you don't know, or no telling as in you're not telling."

"No telling," I repeat.

I talk her into driving up Lock Lane. It goes above the Quarry, and I have her stop at Harper and Simone Simpson's old home. I persuade her to pull into the driveway. I get out, and through the cast-iron fence, I can see the patio, just the way Bitsy described it.

"OK," I say when I get back in the car, putting my hands up to the heater vent.

"OK, what? You have to give me more than this, Willie, if you want me to help you."

So I tell her about the bricks, about what Bitsy Winston-Jones told me.

"That sounds kind of farfetched."

"Yes, it does. But Alicia was afraid of something. She tried to let Bitsy know what it was, and it definitely had something to do with the bricks."

"So, what are you going to do?"

"No telling."

She lets me off at the Prestwould and declines my half-hearted offer for her to come up. Before she leaves, I ask her about the DUI and its possible consequences.

"Do you think you can keep me from having to buy a bicycle?" I ask her, leaning into the open driver's-side window.

"No telling," she says, and drives off.

I walk down to the newspaper and spend some quality time with Sarah, who tells me about her exciting evening on night cops.

"There was this guy," she says, "who they caught stealing a flat-screen TV from Target. Somehow, he got it all the way out of the store with nobody noticing, but he didn't have a getaway car. He had a getaway bus."

"Bus?"

"Yeah. He waited for the city bus, he got on the bus, he left. Several people saw him, but I guess they didn't want to get involved."

"So, did they catch him?"

"Finally. The bus driver who picked him up said he got off at Broad, down by the state library. The driver said he helped him get it off the bus."

"Good samaritan."

"And then some cop in the East End stopped him as he was wrestling it down the street and they finally got him. I talked to the cop, and he said the guy was like one of those little birds you see, trying to carry off a piece of bread as big as he is.

"But it's crazy. He got almost all the way home with it. I mean, a lady phoned Target and told them what happened, that she'd seen this guy get on a city bus right outside the store with one of their flat-screen TVs in a box, and I guess that's how they knew it was missing."

I scratch my head.

"I guess they need to hire more security at Target. If we had full employment, we'd be able to catch the bad guys, or the bad guys would be working and wouldn't have to steal flat-screen TVs. Maybe they ought to hire the bus bandit. Kill two birds with one stone."

"Bus bandit," Sarah says. "That's good. I'll use that."

"You didn't write it for today's paper?"

"Nah. Sally said they were all filled up last night, unless it was a murder or something. I put it on the website, though."

"Of course."

I tell Sarah what she needs to know about Wesley Simpson and the bricks.

"So, you're going to have a look."

"Probably."

I check the weather report. InaccuWeather on A2 says it'll be bright and clear tonight, mostly cloudy tomorrow with a chance of rain or light snow.

Sometime after six, I get Custalow to drive me back to Lock Lane. We sit two doors down from the Simpsons' old place. There's a light on in one of the upstairs windows.

"What do you think?" Custalow says. I've brought him pretty much up to speed on why we're sitting here in the Windsor Farms darkness like a couple of cat burglars.

"I don't know, but there's only one person I can think of who might be in that house tonight."

He nods.

Wesley Simpson should be "resting comfortably" at his sister's home, but that apparently is not the case.

"Maybe," I tell Abe, "I'll wait for the clouds to roll in."

CHAPTER SEVENTEEN

Wednesday

Our weather page nailed it, more or less. Even a broken clock is right twice a day.

It's been cloudy and cold, spitting snow but no accumulation likely. Sitting here in the dark with the heater in my Accord going full blast, I'm almost disappointed not to see a light in any of the windows at the Simpsons' old house. I'm looking for an excuse not to do this. It would be a good night to hunker down in a nice, warm bar. It is, by my reckoning, not a good night to be snooping around somebody else's backyard, armed with a garden trowel.

Custalow has his window open slightly, to let out some of the carcinogens. It's my car and I'll smoke if I want to.

Abe's my chauffeur tonight. Kate's a trouper, but I thought it might be smarter to have someone a little larger and scarier come with me on this little sortie. To my knowledge, Custlow hasn't done physical damage to anyone recently. But the potential is definitely there.

But stealth isn't Abe's strong suit. I'm not sure he can even get over the fence separating me from the brick patio, and it'll be easier for one out-of-shape old fart to do this undetected than it would be for two.

I tell Abe to wait, I'll be right back. We're no more than 100 feet from the start of the circular drive at the front of the house. When Kate drove me up here yesterday, she said it was Georgian, and I told her it did kind of look like some of the houses I'd seen in Atlanta.

"You sure you want to do this?" Abe asks me.

I tell him I am. Actually, I'm not, but what are the choices? I've got less than five days left of the seven Grubby gave me to make chicken salad out of all this. What are the cops going to do if I tell them I think there might be some paper buried maybe somewhere under the brick patio of the late Harper and Simone Simpson's home that might have something to do with their daughter's death. Hell, if I was a cop, I wouldn't put down my doughnut for that. They have a perfectly good suspect, good as it gets, all locked up. Why keep looking?

"Sit," I tell him. "Stay. And keep the heater running. I'm gonna be pretty cold when I get back."

"Nah," he says, and cuts the engine off. He's right, of course. The quieter, the better. The Accord, in need of a tune-up, will be like a neon sign flashing "burglars about" if it sits here idling on this very rich, very private street. The police probably will question Custalow just for being here, if they happen to drive by. It's rare to see a car here at all; most of them are ensconced in garages that are better built than the houses in Oregon Hill. I hope I'm not getting my oldest, most trusted friend into something that will cause an awkward moment with his parole officer.

"I'll be right back," I tell him, and hope I'm right.

I look at the lighted dial on my watch. It's almost nine. It has been a long day.

Peggy phoned while I was still smoking breakfast. She hardly ever calls just to chat. Small and large emergencies occur often enough to make "chat" calls unnecessary.

The news was that Les was missing again. He wasn't there when Peggy got up. He wasn't on the roof, which I took to be a good sign. I hoped he wasn't on anybody's roof, because it wasn't a good morning for climbing on stepladders and scuttering along Oregon Hill rooftops, hoping you didn't step through the rotted-out spot that leaks when it rains.

"It's been almost two hours, and nobody's seen him," she said. I reminded her that I don't at present have a driver's license.

"Well, can't you do something?"

Les doesn't have a car either, unless he's stolen one, so I figured he must be in the general area. To ease my mother's deep-fried mind, I put on my winter coat and a serviceable hat and took the elevator down, en route to the Hill.

Clara Westbrook was in the lobby, waiting for a ride somewhere. "Goodness," she said. "It's not a nice day for a walk, is it?"

I told her it certainly wasn't, but that I was on an idiot hunt.

"Well," she said, "good luck. If you see somebody else outside in this weather, that's probably your man."

I walked through Monroe Park, taking a zigzag course in hopes of finding Les out there somewhere, but not even the most shelter-phobic bum was braving this day outdoors. He didn't show up anywhere along the route to Peggy's.

She let me in, fazed enough that her eyes weren't dilated yet. Awesome had come up from the basement to try to comfort her, but he wasn't doing a very good job of it, reminding her, for some reason, that a homeless guy had frozen to death over by Texas Beach last week.

"But he was way crazier than ol' Les," Awesome added, trying to minimize the damage a bit.

I went out again, this time headed toward the river. Awesome insisted on coming with me, chattering all the way until I told him, as Peggy does in these situations, to shut the fuck up.

We weren't yet to China Street when I looked over and pretty much knew where Les was.

The remains of David Junior Shiflett's burned-out house still had a roof, more or less, and no one has been ordered to level the structure yet. The site of my near-death experience last year still gives me the willies, but I was pretty sure what I was going to find when I got inside. The cold overrode Awesome's fear of the place, and he followed me inside.

Les was sitting on the floor, over where the stairs used to be. I walked over like I was treading on hot coals. Who knew how much weight those fire-damaged timbers could take?

"Les," I said, "don't you think it's time to come home? It's raining a little, and I don't think you're going to get much shelter in here."

Les looked up. You could see gray sky through the holes. Les ran a roofing company after he left baseball.

"Yeah," he said, "I think that roof needs a little work, all right. I don't know if we can save it or not."

He went on about the vagaries of fixing roofs in old, dilapidated buildings as I led him outside, sharing my umbrella. Awesome had a poncho he got from somewhere.

Les looked back at the place where he'd saved my life.

"Sometimes, I come here," he said. "I felt like I was right when I was here."

Maybe Les thinks he can regain his off-and-on grip on sanity in the shell of David Junior Shiflett's house. It kind of makes sense. He never seemed saner than he did the night he broke through that door and pulled me from the flames. Maybe Les can't break out of the fog anymore unless the stakes are so high that he doesn't have any choice.

Either way, I'm glad he was able to see clearly that one night. I will never forget that, and I will never stop looking for him when he wanders off.

"We found him," Awesome announced as we came in, a little worse for the chill and damp, happy to share the coffee Peggy's made. Soon, I smelled the sweet scent of weed and knew my mother was feeling more or less back to normal.

I had promised to take Peggy over to see her granddaughter in the hospital. I was afraid, though, to risk driving. Too many Richmond cops know me, and would be more than pleased to bust my ass over driving with a suspended license.

"I can drive," Les said. I stifled a laugh.

"He's tellin' the truth," Peggy said. "He doesn't have to get his license renewed until year after next. If you tell him where to go, he's a good driver."

The thought that Les had been driving my mother around, in somebody's borrowed car, made me tremble, but I couldn't come up with a better idea.

I told them that Les and I would walk over to the Prestwould to get my Accord, and then come back and pick her up.

Awesome said he would stay and guard the house. I don't think he likes hospitals very much. Who does?

Still, it worked out. Les can still drive OK, with a little direction.

We all went up to Andi's room, and Peggy, not obviously stoned, gave her a big hug. The two of them have always been pretty close. I think my daughter probably sees more of her grandmother than she does of me. Left out of the conversation, Les and I excused ourselves at some point and stepped into the hallway for a while.

As the three of us were leaving, the nurse practitioner pulled me aside and said they probably would be releasing Andi on Friday.

"The mother said you might be taking her."

When did Jeanette tell her that?

"Um, yes. I guess so. But, I mean, will she need special care— you know, special attention?"

"I'm sure she will," the nurse practitioner said. "We'll go over all that with you on Friday."

I nodded my head, unwilling to admit to a stranger that the thought of taking care of my adult daughter somehow freaked me out. I am a liberal arts major, I wanted to tell her. If I had wanted to minister to the sick, I would have taken a biology course or two.

On the way back to the car, I told Peggy what the plan was. She told me, again, that she and Les could take care of Andi.

I told her I was afraid she'd misplace her.

"She won't be the most difficult person I'm taking care of, and at least I want to do it."

I looked at my mother, wondering: Is it that obvious?

"Don't worry," I tell Peggy. "I'm on it."

"You damn sure ought to be."

Coming back meant dropping Peggy off, guiding Les back to the Prestwould parking lot, then walking Les back, lest he forget the way.

When I headed home, it was already two thirty. So I stopped at the 821, had a burger and then, when the food was gone, continued with the longneck Miller High Life's, which are damn near free. I like to go in, slap down a ten dollar bill, and say, "Keep 'em coming."

With nothing to do until tonight except drink and sober up, I went at the former pursuit with some vigor.

It was dark when I stumbled up the steps. The wind had picked up, and the snow peppering my face had an icy feel to it.

Upstairs, I didn't say much to Custalow, just reminded him that he had promised to drive me somewhere.

"When?"

"When I wake up." And I asked him to rouse me at eight. I figured that would be late enough.

∽

I'm glad for the wind and generally nasty conditions. It'll make it easier to do what I mean to do.

I feel like a fool, chasing Bitsy's long-shot hunch. I've learned that long shots seldom pay off. But if you don't bet, you don't win.

So here I am. The Simpsons' old house looks as grand as Monticello in this light. My knowledge of old homes that are only sporadically lived in, though, tells me that a closer inspection would show broken tiles, half-empty rooms and water damage.

I don't intend to do any home inspections tonight, though. I try to make my running shoes as silent as possible as I creep along the driveway, headed for the fence that separates me from the patio. I figure the wind covers what little noise I'm making. There's a streetlight out front. When I get to the fence, I see that someone has left the light on over the back door, but there's no other light either inside the house or out. I won't be in total darkness, but close enough. The red fleece jacket probably wasn't the best idea, but I forgot to change into my burglar's clothes. I can feel the garden trowel sticking out of the pocket of my khakis every time I move.

The fence has nothing on the outside for me to boost myself up with. The gate is locked, like I figured it would be, but I'm finally able to get something of a toehold by putting one foot on the lower hinge. I wonder if I'm providing Custalow with his night's entertainment as I swing one leg up and, on the third try, am able to rather painfully straddle the fence. A minute or so more, and I'm inside, doing a half-gainer into the garden as my trailing foot catches on the top of the gate.

I brush the dirt off me and unlock the latch, then wait a few seconds to let my eyes adjust to the dark. Only the back-door light gives me any illumination at all, and its range stops well short of where I know the brick patio is.

Moving forward a step at a time, I find the patio with my feet. By now, I can see a little bit, and it takes me only a couple more minutes to find the loose bricks Bitsy told me about.

I pry one of them up with the trowel, then the other one. At first, there doesn't appear to be anything but West End mud underneath. But then I dig a little and feel something that doesn't give. After scraping away the mud, I reach down and feel plastic. A penlight would have been another good thing to have brought along tonight.

It doesn't take long to unearth it. It could be what Alicia Parker Simpson buried there in the recent past, or it could be plastic-wrapped Nancy Drew books from 1980.

I pull it out, and then stand stiffly as the ice pelts me with a little more enthusiasm. It could be little Alicia Simpson's seventh-grade term paper, but it's definitely paper, and a fair amount of it.

Mission accomplished, I'm saying to myself, when I turn and come very close to losing control of my sphincter muscles.

How Wesley Simpson got that close to me without me hearing is a mystery. I suppose the wind, my alleged friend, was just as good at covering the sounds of Wes's footsteps as I thought it was at covering mine.

"What are you doing?" he asks. He seems calm. I can barely hear him over the wind. It wouldn't be as spooky, I'm thinking, if he was yelling and screaming. I can feel the snow hitting my face. My eyes have adjusted well enough to the darkness that I can see him now. He looks every bit as out of it as he did at the funeral, the last time I saw him.

He has a shovel in his right hand, as if he has come to help me dig. I start to answer when he brings the shovel around, faster than I would have thought possible for a man who's supposed to be on mind-numbing anti-psychotics.

"You were looking for something," he says. There's a gash in the side of my face, and my left ear's ringing like a damn phone.

There's nothing much I can say to that. I'm crawling around his parents' patio, digging up the bricks, and I have five pounds of plastic-wrapped contraband in my hand. Busted.

It doesn't appear to me, though, that Wesley is interested in calling the police. He seems to have something more immediate and permanent in mind. He seems to want to dispatch me the same way he'd take care of a mole that was digging up his garden.

I partially ward off his second blow with my left arm, but I'm knocked on my side by the force of it. Wesley has quite an impressive swing for a guy who probably hasn't played baseball in a while.

I'm greatly outgunned here, with nothing but my little garden spade, which I'm still gripping in my right hand. I notice that Wesley is wearing bedroom slippers in the cold February night. I guess Lewis and Carl have been letting him stay over here since he was shipped back from Arkansas. Better than having him at their place—for them, at least.

He's standing over me, and he's lifting that big shovel over his head when I do the only thing I can think of that might save my butt.

The spade isn't as good as a knife, but it does have a point at the end, and when I drive it into the top of Wesley Simpson's left foot, I can feel little bones cracking. That's got to hurt.

He howls and falls to his knees. I drop the spade, hang on to my plastic-protected treasure and try to get the hell out of there.

My legs are working OK, although my left arm is numb, making it hard to get up. I can feel blood rolling down my face. I push myself up with my right arm and I'm making the transition from prone to running for my life, when Wesley grabs my ankle. I kick his face hard enough to make him let go and scramble for the gate. The fact that I left it unlocked probably makes the difference. He's limping toward me, screaming, using that damn shovel like a crutch, but he's too late.

I'm out the driveway, up the street and back in the car in Olympic record time. Custalow has started the engine before I even get there, sensing some urgency in my bloodied face. As we speed past the Simpson house, I see Wesley coming across the front yard at a forty-five-degree angle from us, running hard like a dog chasing a car, waving the shovel. He gets close, and then I hear a thump as we pass him. I'm afraid we've hit him, but when I turn around, I see him standing there, and the shovel is spinning around in the road. He must have thrown it when he realized he wasn't going to catch us.

Back at the Prestwould parking lot, Custalow wipes my face as clean as he can with his handkerchief and has me put on his jacket—which is not covered with blood—while I carry mine.

"You might scare the guard," he says, referencing the VCU kid who'll be sleeping at the front desk when we come in. I appreciate that Abe isn't asking any questions. I don't mind answering questions, but my face hurts. When I look at the right side of the car, there's a dent, compliments of Wesley's shovel. I wonder if he's left one on my head, too.

We get up to the sixth floor, and I collapse in the Eames chair. Kate's going to be really pissed that the carpet probably has blood on it now.

"Looks like you got it," Custalow says.

"What?"

He nods at my right hand.

I look down and see that I'm still gripping what I just took a major beat-down to get.

"Happy reading," Abe says. "I hope it was worth it."

A couple of Advils later, I realize that I never even thanked him for risking his freedom to help me chase some half-assed hunch.

CHAPTER EIGHTEEN

Thursday

I was up most of the night, reading.

Alicia wasn't the greatest writer. At least, she wasn't when she interned for us all those years ago. But what I've just read wasn't bad. Once you picked it up, you just couldn't put it down.

It didn't take me long to get the gist of what had happened. I fell asleep sometime after three.

Now it's just after nine, and I'm wide awake, sitting in the living room, watching the hawk atop his tree. He seems to be contemplating a little late breakfast. There's a knot on the side of my head big enough that, when I look in the mirror, my noggin looks lopsided. My jaw aches and my shoulder hurts like a bitch. Wesley Simpson swings a mean shovel.

First, I call Grubby. My earnest, hard-working publisher has probably been in his office for three or four hours already. Grubby seems to think that, if he works hard enough, he can undo the damage technology and illiteracy have done to print journalism. Or at least convince people who have been reading us for free online for several years that they now should pay for the privilege. Good one. There isn't one honest journalist I know who ever, and I mean ever, thought giving it away was a good idea. But we don't have MBAs. What the fuck do we know?

Normally, it wouldn't be possible to reach James H. Grubbs by simply picking up the phone and calling. However, when I tell Sandy McCool who it is (and apologize for my recent invasion of the publisher's office), and that I have news Grubby's going to want to hear—or at least that he needs to hear, right now—she puts me through. Sandy, at least, trusts my instincts.

"Willie," Grubby says. It almost sounds as if he's stifling a yawn. I suggest that he needs more sleep.

"No, I can get by on four hours a night. Been doing it for years. What I need is for drunk, suspended reporters to not interrupt my workday. DUI? On Franklin Street, practically in front of the building? Really?"

Word gets around. I tell him that I'm not making a social call.

"What's this, Thursday? Four more days, Willie."

It almost sounds like he'd rather fire me than have a great story.

Before he can hang up and chastise Sandy for not screening his calls better, I cut to the chase. I tell him only the basic stuff, just enough to let him know that, Giles Whitehurst and the disapprobation of the West End notwithstanding, we have a tiger by the tail. If the paper has a hair on its scrawny ass, it will have to proceed. We've crawled into a tight little hole, and the only way out is to go forward, toward the pinprick of light at the other end.

"You're sure it's hers?"

"It has to be. She told her friend where it would be if anything happened. And it was right there."

"Did anybody see you?"

I hesitate, then prevaricate a bit.

"The brother. Wesley. He must be staying there. At least he was last night. But he couldn't identify me. It was too dark." Not sure about that one. I'm thinking that Wesley Simpson is probably in a fair amount of pain right now. As much as I'm in, I hope. I'm not sure what a concussion feels like, but if I was playing football and took a hit like the one Wesley gave me with that shovel, the trainer might be asking me what day it was. But I can't swear that ol' Wes can't identify me.

"So," Grubby says, "none of this really proves anything, does it?"

"Not if you take it a piece at a time. But if you add Alicia's call to Susan Winston-Jones and what I read last night to Bump Freeman's phone call and Richard Slade's record of nonviolence over the past twenty-eight years, don't you start shading over into 'reasonable doubt' territory?"

"A court can decide that."

I remind Grubby that everybody let a court do the deciding twenty-eight years ago, and all it got Richard Slade was a life sentence.

He's quiet for a few seconds.

"OK," he says at last. "Let me make a call."

"To Giles Whitehurst?"

"Let me make a call."

After I hang up, I ponder my options. Play it safe and wait for Grubby to get a yea or nay from the chairman of the board and arbiter of what's appropriate in Windsor Farms, or call Lewis Simpson Witt.

Screw it. Like I told Grubby, we have to wriggle our way forward. No going back.

To my surprise, Lewis herself answers.

I identify myself and, before she can hang up, I tell her what I've spent much of last night reading.

After a long silence, one that I have to force myself not to break, knowing like any good reporter that the other party will eventually speak, she says, "Alicia told me, shortly before her death, that she was trying her hand at fiction."

I tell Lewis that I don't think so.

"I don't really care what you think, Mr. Black. I suppose this is why my brother is limping around the house. He said he surprised an intruder at my parents' home last night. It pleases me to think that I won't have to worry about anonymous strangers disturbing our peace. Case closed, as they say. Expect a visit from the police. Soon."

"Again, I don't think so."

Lewis is furious and trying not to show it.

"And why is that?" she says.

"Because I believe every word I read there. I was told that she was afraid. She told a friend days before that something might happen, and where she could find the manuscript."

"Bitsy!"

Uh-oh. Me and my big mouth.

"I don't reveal sources."

I hear what sounds like a chuckle, albeit a mirthless one. "Oh, but you do, Mr. Black. You do."

"At any rate," I go on, "do you have any response to what I've just told you, before we write about it?"

"You won't be writing about anything. And if somehow you do, I'll own that goddamn newspaper. I'll sue you so hard you'll have to move back in with your white trash Oregon Hill mother. Hell, I'll sue her, too, just for having you."

"Somebody's been doing her homework."

"Mr. Black," she says, "it pays to know your enemy."

I try to protest that I'm not really her enemy, just an honest reporter trying to do his job, but she cuts me off.

"You want to talk? All right, we'll talk. Come here tomorrow night, seven o'clock. Don't be late. I'll tell you a story, Mr. Black."

I'm surprised that Lewis is willing to talk with me under any circumstances, but I'm a little concerned about my apparent good luck.

I ask if we can make it earlier, or somewhere else. No dice. Seven at her place it is.

She hangs up before I even have a chance to say goodbye.

Next call is to Kate. I fill her in, at least as far as telling her I have Alicia Simpson's manuscript, diary, journal, whatever. I ask if we can have a chat with Richard Slade. She says she'll check with Marcus. I have a feeling that she's giving Green and Slade's case as much time as she's ever given BB&B.

She calls back in five minutes and says we can meet with Slade at two. It's after noon, and I ask her if she's eaten yet. She has a meeting at one and begs off.

"One other thing," she says as I'm about to hang up. "Slade said he saw somebody."

"Saw somebody when?"

"That night. Back in 1983. He said he told the cops at the time, but they didn't really want to hear it, I'm sure, and his half-assed lawyer never brought it up at the trial. Just trying to keep him from frying, I guess."

"He saw somebody, like at the Quarry?"

"Yeah. But I'll let him tell you."

She hangs up before I can ask her anything more.

I do a raid on the refrigerator and am uninspired by the two hot dogs that look to be past their due date, and one lonely egg and cheddar cheese that is turning a lovely color of blue-green. Custalow and I don't so much shop as forage for groceries, going out for what we might need in the immediate future, and it's obvious that neither of us has gone out lately.

Abe comes up while I'm staring into the abyss.

"How you doing?" he asks, and I'm touched that he came up here just to make sure I haven't died. I tell him fine, better than our food supply.

I persuade him to take a slightly longer than usual lunch break and come with me to Perly's. He can drive, saving me a walk I'd rather forgo. My head tells me it's Advil time again. And then he can drop me off at the city jail.

"Sure," he says.

On the way, I see Awesome Dude, ambling along Grace Street. It might be the eighties. The Dude is a perennial.

I tell Custalow to pull over, and I ask Awesome if he'd like to join us for lunch.

"Are you paying?"

When he hears the right answer, he hops in.

When we get to Perly's, Abe asks me if I'm OK.

"Dude," Awesome says, "you look like shit."

I'm not offering Custalow any of the gory details of last night's reading—not yet anyhow—and I appreciate that he doesn't ask.

After lunch, Awesome heads for the homeless shelter on Grace. He likes to stay in touch with his old friends. Then Abe takes me to the city lockup. I assure him that I can get a ride back or take the bus.

Kate and Marcus are waiting out front. Kate compliments me for being on time "for a change," then notices that I'm a little the worse for wear. I tell her it's the price I pay for being a snoop.

"So I hear you've got some good news for our client," Marcus says.

"Nothing that's going to stand up in court."

"I'm just looking for something that'll make him feel like breathing again. He hasn't eaten a damn thing in the last two days, or so they tell me."

I assure him that this won't make his client feel any worse, but I don't want to get Richard Slade's hopes up just to have them squashed like a bug. He's had more than enough of that.

When we're all seated, Richard there in shackles, I tell him that I've come across some information that gives us (meaning me) reason to believe someone else might have killed Alicia Parker Simpson.

Richard looks me in the eye. He seems like he's lost about ten pounds he didn't need to lose.

"Man," he says, so quietly that I have to lean forward to hear him, "I thought you knew that. Tell me something I don't know."

"I mean," I tell him, "I've got something that might make somebody other than your mother or us in this room believe it, but I've still got some work to do."

I tell him about the diary, without revealing all the gory details.

"Now, you tell me something I don't know. Tell me about that night. Back in 1983."

He knows what I'm talking about.

"I told the cops that night, and I told my lawyer. Fat lot of good it did me. And it might have been nothing. All I know is, I remember, when we heard the cop car coming and we were scrambling and all, trying to get out of there, I saw something. Somebody."

"Who?"

"I don't know. But there was footsteps, going fast, and I just got a glimpse of a guy running off into the dark. He wasn't under the light but for a second or two, but I know somebody else was there. I told the cops that, but nobody listened. They had what they wanted already, I guess."

"White guy?" I ask him.

He nods.

"None of this is going to prove anything about Alicia Simpson's death," I tell him. "It might even make some jury think, 'Hell, if it was me, I'd've killed her too.' But it's something to build on. That plus the phone call might carry some weight."

Richard Slade doesn't say anything for what seems like a minute, and none of us do, either.

Then he clears his throat.

"All I can do," he says, "is tell the truth. That's what I've always done."

He turns to me.

"Will you tell my mother? About all this? I think she might need a little cheering up."

I promise him that I will and remind him that Philomena seems like she can handle a lot.

"She's all I've had," he says, "until you all."

"Just do one more thing for me," I tell Richard. "Look me in the eye, right now, and tell me you did not kill Alicia Simpson. I know your life is riding on this, but my livelihood is, too."

He fixes me with an evil-eye stare. He makes it simple.

"I did not kill Alicia Simpson. I don't know anything about who might've killed her. I was in my mother's house when it happened."

There's not much else left to say. Marcus tells him to keep his chin up "and eat something, goddammit."

On the way out, Marcus asks me if I really think I'm about to shake something loose, and I tell him that I'm going to give it my best shot.

"Are you going to tell me what's in that diary of hers?"

All in good time, I assure him.

I walk with Kate to her car. She's willing to drive me home, even if she is, as usual, steamed about my unwillingness to share my feelings, or Alicia Simpson's revelations, with her.

"How are you fixed for time?" I ask her.

She tells me she has a little work back at the office. She's doing some stuff for BB&B, even though she's on leave.

"Doing pro bono work for a law firm?"

"I'm hoping they don't make my little furlough permanent."

I tell her I know how that feels, then ask her if she would like to meet Philomena Slade.

She surprises me by saying that, yes, she believes she would.

The ride out to Philomena's takes maybe ten minutes. She's keeping the twins, as usual. Jamal and Jeroy stop harassing a feral cat out in the front yard long enough to tell me that Momma Phil is inside. The boys know me by now, and Kate goes out of her way to make nice with them. She's good with kids and ought to have some herself.

Philomena lets us in. I'm thankful she doesn't mention that I look like shit. I introduce Kate, who within two minutes compliments her on her dress, the decor of her living room and the smells emanating from the kitchen.

"Chicken and pastry," Philomena says. "The boys like it. It was Richard's favorite. I was going to fix it for him, but . . ."

She turns away. Kate, who is somewhat more of a people person than me, is by her side with her arm around her as if Philomena were her own aunt.

"We're going to make this right," she says, and I add that when Kate decides she's going to make something right, it usually turns out that way.

I tell Philomena about what Alicia wrote, or at least a lot of it. I also tell her that it very well could have some bearing on how and by whom Alicia was murdered. Kate is staring daggers, no doubt wondering why I'm sharing something with this woman that I didn't deign to share with her and Marcus Green earlier.

"Well," Philomena says, wiping her eyes, "I'm glad to hear you don't think it was Richard. I'm glad somebody does."

I assure her that I've never thought anything else, and I'm only lying a little.

Like any half-assed cops reporter, I've had to dodge flying bullshit on many occasions as criminals—convicted and otherwise—try to enlist me in their hopeless causes. And they are almost always lying.

I am convinced, though, that Richard Slade is not lying. And it has nothing to do with the fact that he's my cousin. It's just that all those heartrending pleas from con artists lying through their teeth have given me, or at least I think so, a feel for that rarest of gems: cold, hard truth.

Part of it is mannerisms—no blinking or nervous tics or hand gestures. Part of it is a dearth of b.s. preludes: "I'll tell you the truth," "truthfully," "to be honest about it," "true story," and so on. But mostly it's just a feeling you get when that rare wronged honest man looks you in the eye and says, "I did not do it."

Philomena invites us to stay for supper, and I'm tempted. Peggy's house never smelled this good. But Kate has to get back.

Before we can leave, the boys' mother, Chanelle, drives up. She's going to have dinner with her aunt tonight. I've never met Chanelle before. She's a lovely young woman with a 100-watt smile, thin despite the boys, or maybe because of them. She works for the DMV and is taking courses at the community college. I tell her I hope we can get together again, when we can talk longer. She calls me "cousin" and says she hopes so, too.

As Philomena walks us to the door, Kate turns to me and says, "I wish you'd introduced me to this lady when we were married."

Philomena stops.

"You two were married?"

I explain, as much as I can as quickly as I can, about our ill-fated union. I can feel that I'm blushing. Kate stands to one side wearing an amused half-smile.

"Well," Philomena says, "you all ought to give it another try. You look good together."

We both thank her for what seems to be a compliment.

In the car, Kate tells me that I might have shared my Cliffs-Notes version of Alicia Simpson's diary with her and Marcus earlier.

I shrug.

"I thought Philomena might need a little encouragement."

I ask Kate if she'd like to go somewhere for a bite.

She says she has to go home.

I ask her where exactly home is.

"Home is home," she says.

It takes me a second or two.

"The home that also houses Mr. Ellis?"

"The same."

There's an awkward silence.

"Willie," she says, putting her right hand on my arm while steering around an impressive pothole with her left, "I've been meaning to tell you. Greg and I are trying to make it work again. We're trying to have . . . I don't know why I'm telling you this . . . we're trying to have a baby."

I'm a little surprised and a little sad. Not just for me, although I have harbored hopes of late that Kate might somehow turn out to be my third AND fourth wife. But I feel a little twinge for her, too. She's always trying, and it seems like she shouldn't have to try so much. Trying to make her second marriage work. Trying to have a career and keep hubby happy at the same time. Trying to have a baby. I have this image of her the way she used to look when she was concentrating on some sleeping pill of a law book and didn't know I was looking at her: eyes squinched up, chewing on her pen, her forehead creased with a frown line that I would try to make disappear with my fingers. Kate is always trying.

I wish her good luck when I get out.

She starts to say something, but then thinks better of it and drives off into the fading light.

Clara Westbrook is in the lobby when I walk in.

She, like just about everyone else today, asks about why my head looks like somebody used it for batting practice.

I tell her I fell. It probably would just depress her to know that her godson was the batter.

"Looks like you fell two or three times," she says.

Upstairs, Custalow tells me I had a call. He hands me the name and number.

Giles Whitehurst.

I guess I've pissed the chairman off enough that he wants to eliminate the middleman and fire me personally.

It's a call I'd rather not make for a while, say until hell freezes over, but it's going to be hard to eat or sleep until I do the deed.

"Whitehurst residence," an unctuous voice answers.

When I tell the butler or whoever the fuck answers Giles Whitehurst's phone who it is, he says, "Just a moment, please," and it seems almost like I can hear him chuckle as he goes to deliver the news to his master.

A few seconds later, Whitehurst is there, probably holding his bourbon glass in his free hand.

"Yes?"

I explain that I'm returning his call.

"Ah, yes," he says, as if he's totally forgotten, in the chaos of his busy day, that he was supposed to ream out and then fire a reporter. "Mr. Black. Yes. I, um, wanted to talk to you about this whole Alicia Simpson business."

I'm silent.

"The thing is, the family has been through quite a lot lately, and I would really appreciate it, as a personal favor, if you would drop the matter. The police seem to have things well in hand without your help."

I should just shut up, but I gotta be me.

"I'm not so sure they have the right man in jail."

"So I've heard," Giles Whitehurst says, with perhaps a bit more edge, a little steel poking up through the silk. "But let's just wait until after the trial. Let justice run its course."

"I'm not so sure justice is running its course."

I hear a sigh and the tinkle of ice cubes.

"Mr. Black, I'm not sure you understand what I'm saying. This isn't exactly a request."

Well, why didn't you say so? Here I thought it was just a multi-millionaire who's chairman of the board of the company that owns me asking me for a pretty-please favor.

"I understand."

"And although I haven't talked with Lewis in a couple of days, I'm sure she would be very grateful if you were to back off a bit."

"Do I have a choice?"

"No, Mr. Black, you don't, other than unemployment."

When I don't speak, he says, "Are we in agreement?"

I tell him we are, and he hangs up.

I'm halfway to the living room when it hits me. Giles Whitehurst hasn't talked with Lewis since I talked to her. Which means she hasn't called him to complain about my latest round of meddling.

Which means she hasn't seen fit to tell him about our meeting tomorrow night.

Which means, hell or high water, I'm going. There are some things, it seems, that Lewis Witt doesn't want the chairman to know about. Just me.

I'm watching an *Everyone Loves Raymond* rerun and trying not to think of bourbon when I get the call from Jeanette.

"They're releasing her first thing in the morning," my first wife says. "You should be here by nine."

Andi. Shit. I'd forgotten all about my daughter. I'm too tired and ashamed to come up with some lame-ass excuse as to why I can't, finally, do something helpful for Andi.

"I'll be there," I tell her. "Glad to do it."

CHAPTER NINETEEN

Friday

The Witts don't seem to mind wasting electricity. It looks like every light in the place is on.

The old Tudor glowers down at me, daring me to approach it. It's bone-deep cold, one of those nights that make you count the hours until the Red Sox head for spring training. One year about this time, between marriages, I got up on a day like this and started driving south until I smelled spring. I think I was outside of Lakeland, Florida, before that happened. Which made it all the colder when I turned around and came back.

I look at my watch: 6:55. I don't want to appear overeager, but I'm freezing my ass off. Besides, she had to hear the Honda straining its way up the drive.

Custalow wanted to chauffeur me here, but I told him that wasn't the deal. I was to come alone, even if it meant defying the law by driving myself. It felt kind of funny to be behind the wheel again.

Before I left, he put his big bear paw on my shoulder and told me to be careful, and to call him if anything went wrong. I told him not to worry. What was a West End matron going to do to me?

Then I kissed Andi on the cheek and told her I'd see her soon. She doesn't know much about what her idiot father is doing, which is the way I want it.

Misgivings? I have a few. But I didn't come unarmed. I have my tape recorder.

I push the buzzer. A few seconds later, Lewis Witt opens the door. I think at first I've come at the wrong time, because she seems to be dressed for a party. Pearls, little black dress, heels. The works.

"Come in, Mr. Black," she says. "I've been expecting you."

Custalow and I brought Andi home this morning. We were at the hospital by eight thirty, just in case. Hospitals being hospitals, we finally made our escape sometime after eleven, after they had schooled me on what signs might indicate that my daughter's concussion was worse than they thought. I apologized to Abe for costing him half a day's work. He told me to shut up.

Andi had a cast on her left arm and looked like somebody had used her for a punching bag. I probably didn't look much better. One of the smart-ass nurses asked me who was going to be taking care of whom.

When they finally released her, she refused to let them roll her out to the car in a wheelchair. As we made our way slowly down the endless corridors between us and freedom, Andi looked at me and laughed.

"We look like the walking wounded," she said.

"At least we're walking."

She has always gone a mile a minute. Jeanette thought for a while she had ADHD, but she's just enthusiastic. And so, it was a bit of a shock to see how slowly she was moving. Three times, I had to stop when I realized I was leaving her behind in my eagerness to get out of that damn hospital.

Custalow had gone ahead to get the car, probably as glad as me to be back in well-world. It occurred to me that we could have gotten there maybe five times quicker if we'd accepted the wheelchair ride, but I appreciate Andi's independence, her refusal to lie down. If I'd been in her place, in a hospital for six days, I'd have done it just like she did.

Back at the Prestwould, Grace Montross and Louisa Barron were in the lobby and made a big fuss over Andi. Through the grapevine, they'd heard about her accident. She endured the attention, even smiling slightly. They assured me that they would be checking in on her. The way the Prestwould works, I was pretty certain that Abe and I wouldn't have to worry about fixing dinner for the next few nights.

I had changed the sheets so Andi could have the master bedroom. The trundle bed in the study would be my resting place until she was OK to be on her own. She objected, said she didn't want to be a bother. I told her she was my princess, and the princess should always get the best bed.

"You used to call me that," she said. "When I was little."

We talked some, about nothing much. The guard Andi usually has up when I'm trying to act like an actual father was down a bit. Nothing like getting half-killed in a wreck to make you vulnerable.

She said she was a little tired, so I helped her into bed. I leaned over to tuck her in and kissed her on her forehead. Over the years, we've hugged when meeting or departing from each other's company, and I've slipped a stray kiss or two onto her cheeks, but shows of affection aren't Andi's thing—at least where her delinquent dad is concerned.

Today, though, she looked at me and said, "Thank you, Daddy."

It made sleeping on the trundle bed more than worth it.

After Andi drifted off, I called Sarah Goodnight. I gave her a progress report.

"You're going over there tonight? No shit?"

I assured her that I had indeed arranged a meeting with Lewis Witt.

"Man," Sarah said, "you must really have her spooked. She hates your ass."

I told Sarah that she needed to watch her language. She told me she's been spending too much time around journalists. Then she asked me when we might be able to write something about this for the paper.

"Maybe never," I told her, relating the high points of my conversation with the chairman of the board.

"But if it's good enough, we'll write it anyway, right?"

I told her, yeah, but we have to get the paper to run it, and it has to be good enough to make it worth getting fired over.

"No prob," Sarah said. "I can always get another job."

"I'm not thinking about you." Well, maybe a little.

"Oh, you'll be fine."

The confidence of youth is amazing. I used to have that. The newborn lamb does not fear the lion, and all that shit.

"Can I come with you?" Sarah asked.

I tell her that's out of the question. Lewis made it clear that she would only talk to me, alone.

"Lucky you."

"I hope so."

I spent much of the day looking after Andi, who napped on and off and gobbled down the BLT I made her for lunch. I hovered so much that she finally asked me, nicely, if she could just be left alone for a little bit. She doesn't need that much assistance, but having only one working arm does present problems.

When she had to go to the bathroom and I offered to help, she told me that she would have to be a lot worse off than she was now for that to be an option.

Late in the afternoon, I got a call from Susan Winston-Jones. Before I could even tell Bitsy that her hunch about the bricks was right, she started in on me.

"She knows," is how she began the conversation. "How the hell does she know?"

It didn't take me long to deduce that "she" was Lewis Witt, and what she knew was that Bitsy had been talking to me.

I apologized, explaining how I had inadvertently mentioned that I knew about Alicia's manuscript because a friend had told me about it.

"And she figured right away that the friend was you."

"You didn't tell her it was me? Then how did she figure it out?"

I wanted to say that maybe Bitsy was the only one of Alicia's friends who might have felt compelled to tell a stranger about it. Or maybe she was Alicia's only friend.

"Lucky guess," I said.

"Well, she knows. She called me every name she could think of. She scared me."

"Scared you? How?"

"She said that she wouldn't forget. Forgive or forget."

"OK, so you have to live with somebody giving you the cold shoulder. You'll survive."

"You don't understand. You don't know Lewis."

I was quiet. She continued.

"Let me tell you a story."

When Lewis was a teenager, Bitsy told me, she was madly in love—or thought she was—with a young man, a member of her group with a rather impressive Roman numeral after his name.

One day, the boy told her it was over. He didn't want to go steady anymore.

"I knew his family, they lived four houses down from us. My older sister, Elizabeth, was just a year behind Lewis at St. Catherine's, and she hung out with the boy's sister. One day, Liz let me tag along with her when she went over there. It was an early summer morning, and we had our bathing suits. We were going down to the Quarry.

"But when we got there, Bobby, that was the boy's name, and his sister and his mother were all standing there at the edge of the driveway. It was early. I remember the dew was still heavy.

"What they were looking down at, lying half-hidden inside the boxwood hedge, cold and dead, was Dabney."

Dabney was Bobby's Labrador retriever. He'd had her since he was in second grade. The dog had gone missing the day before. They'd walked all around the neighborhood, but couldn't find her anywhere. Bobby's father hadn't noticed her body when he went to work that morning, and so it was left to the kids to find her. Her collar was missing, but it was obvious that it was Dabney.

When the vet took her away and did a doggie autopsy, he determined she had been poisoned.

"I was ten or eleven. Liz pulled me away, and we went back home. The whole thing with Dabney was a real shock. Nothing like that ever happened in Windsor Farms. There was talk of neighborhood watches or hiring private security. But then it died down.

"A month or so later, though, we were at the Simpsons' for a party. I wandered away and started exploring. It felt kind of wicked, you know, to be in somebody else's house like that, just snooping."

Somehow, she said, she wound up in Lewis's room.

"I was just going around, opening drawers and stuff. I could hear the adults and the kids off in the distance, mostly out by the pool. Anybody could have walked by."

She said there was a desk, where Lewis probably did her homework.

"I opened the drawer underneath the desktop, and there, with all the pens and pencils and such, was a collar. A dog collar. And you know whose name was on it?"

Didn't take a genius to figure that one out.

"Dabney."

"Yeah. You know, I never told anybody about it, not until I went to college. And nobody in Windsor Farms. To this day. It's about the only secret I've ever kept, I guess.

"But I've always been afraid of Lewis, since then."

Well, I told Bitsy, that was a long time ago.

Bitsy's laugh is as sharp and dry as a good martini.

"People," she said, "don't change."

So here I stand. Lewis Witt leads me into what seems to be an otherwise empty house.

"I understand," she says when we're seated in the living room, which is about the size of my whole apartment, "that you have some information."

I nod. Then, I spell out what I've learned, what Alicia wrote, giving her the short version.

She sits quietly as I tell her what I think happened twenty-eight years ago.

She seems less than shocked.

"I thought there might have been something," she says. "And I just didn't want to know. The sad truth is, both my brother and sister have had issues."

Then I tell her what I think might have happened on January 22nd.

"That's quite a story, Mr. Black," she says when I finish my spiel. "Complete fiction, because my brother has trouble planning what he's going to wear, let alone a murder, but quite a story nonetheless. Do you think anyone will believe it?"

I tell her anyone who read the whole manuscript and knew all the facts might.

"Did you bring it with you?"

I assure her that Alicia's papers are in a safe place.

She sighs, then begins talking.

"Mr. Black, my family has been through a lot. My brother's, ah, illness probably took years off my parents' lives. Then, the rape— or whatever you wish to call it—diminished Alicia in ways you cannot imagine. And then, to be killed the way she was. What's left of my family would like a little peace. We don't exactly need this embarrassment on top of all the grief. I would like very much for that manuscript to never see the light of day."

"Well," I tell her, "I'm not trying to ruin your lives. But there's this guy who's about to spend the rest of his days in prison, if he's allowed to live, and I don't think he did it. Either time."

I see Lewis's lips twitch, almost like she's going to smile. But she doesn't.

"And what, Mr. Black, are these other 'facts' you mentioned?"

I tell her about Bump Freeman and the phone call.

"OK, so suppose this, this man . . ."

"Richard Slade."

"Suppose Richard Slade did answer the phone at his mother's home. What would have kept him from hiring someone else to kill my sister?"

Nothing, I tell her, except there's not one scrap of evidence to indicate that. A gun with no serial number or fingerprints on it. No witnesses. Could have been anyone.

"Seems like a long haul," I tell Lewis, "from there to 'guilty.'"

"Well, we'll let the courts decide that one. But one thing at a time. About that manuscript."

My head's been on a swivel since I got here. I wonder if Wesley is lurking somewhere, waiting to pay me back for Wednesday night.

"Where is your brother, by the way?"

She pauses for a moment.

"Oh, don't worry," she says. "He's not here. And he's not over at Momma and Daddy's, either. He won't be staying there anymore.

"As a matter of fact, Mr. Black, it's just you and me here, all alone. It's Carl's poker night, and my son's spending the night with some friends."

She walks over to a desk, an old, scarred one that stands out like a bottle of Ripple in a wine bar. It looks like it might have belonged to a schoolgirl at one time.

She pulls out a piece of paper. When she gets closer, I see that it's a certified check. Made out to me, with a very large number on it. Holy shit. What Lewis is offering is about the size of my 401(k) before it turned into a 201(k).

"You've worked very hard to get that manuscript, Mr. Black. Some might say you stole it, that you were a snoop who deserves to be arrested for trespassing and assault on a mentally ill man.

"But let's not quibble. I'm willing to let bygones be bygones and just call this a reward for a job well done."

"And you get the manuscript."

"You're very sharp, Mr. Black."

It's tempting. Jackson says everybody's a whore; we just have different prices.

The trouble is, I've pretty much promised the esteemed James H. Grubbs a story that will make me worth the trouble of paying my salary. And I really do like going to work every day. The last week has taught me that if nothing else. The newspaper, which has on occasion beaten and flayed me like Gunga Din on a bad day, might be the only thing between me and a bottomless bottle.

I tell her I can't do it.

"So what will you do with the information?"

"I don't know. I haven't decided."

I really haven't. There's still a lot of bullshit to sort out here. Even if it happened all those years ago the way Alicia wrote it, how can you prove that neither Richard Slade nor an agent of his killed her, just for spite. I know what I know, and I know what I can prove, and the two aren't quite aligned.

Lewis Witt walks over and puts the check back in the drawer. Then she turns toward me.

"Mr. Black," she says, "if you will come with me, I believe I can show you something that will ease your doubts at last about who killed my sister."

"Come where?"

"Just a short drive. This won't take long, I assure you."

I explain that I have a daughter recuperating back at the Prestwould, and I have to get back to check on her.

"Well, if you want to know what really happened, this is your chance."

What choice do I have?

CHAPTER TWENTY

Nov. 22, 2010

I never meant to write this, never wanted to write it. Dr. Burstein wanted me to put everything down on paper a long time ago. He finally dropped me as a patient. Maybe he didn't want to share my guilt. And when I told my father that I felt much better, they just let the whole thing drop. I had had two years of treatment by then, once a week spilling everything to Dr. Burstein. My parents were never very comfortable with psychiatrists. It was against their beliefs—more to the point, their belief that we were perfect.

People are able to tuck things away in the back of the closet, eventually almost forgetting about them. I suppose all those years I had hoped, even convinced myself, that Richard Slade had died in prison, God help me. I'd talked myself into believing that he was just a train wreck waiting to happen, that if it hadn't been my case, it would have been something else, some other girl.

But then somebody broke the code, came up with DNA, and everything that was tucked away in the darkest corner of that long-forgotten closet came tumbling out.

Everybody assumed that I'd just made a mistake, identified the wrong black boy. It had happened, still does, I suppose.

Only three other people know my shame, two really since Dr. Burstein is now dead. And I don't believe it is possible for anyone to know the stain I bear. It is not possible now to even look in a mirror any longer than it takes to ensure that I am at least moderately presentable.

Last week, I went out with only one earring on. Bitsy had to point it out to me.

I have sinned. I don't even believe anymore that there is a God, but there is still sin. And I have wallowed in it and I'm covered with its slime.

What I want to do is get clean again, the way I once was. It may not be possible, but I intend to try.

I intend to keep writing, night and day, until it is all told, until I have vomited up all that I have done.

Since it happened, Lewis has tried to "talk some sense" into me. She tells me that, for the sake of the family, I must keep everything hidden. Who will gain, she asks me, if I tell everything now? Who will lose?

I tell her that she is right, but she seems to doubt my sincerity.

Now, when it seems certain that Richard Slade, whose name I blocked out for so long, will be a free man again soon, walking the streets in the same city, perhaps coming face to face with me eventually, those kind eyes I see in the newspaper stories quietly asking me why, I can no longer stay quiet. The lie within me is too large to contain any longer.

As my Sunday school teacher told us when I was six years old, the truth will out. . . .

Nov. 29

It is time to talk about Wesley.

He was my hero, always there to defend me if anyone tried to pick on me, always patiently showing me the way, helping me with my homework, including me in things when his friends might have thought I was a brat. Two years age difference is a lot when you're ten or twelve.

He was handsome, talented and popular. Yes, I had a crush on my brother.

It seemed innocent enough. He'd show me how to kiss, tell me what to look out for from the older boys, even though, at twelve, I wasn't turning any heads. We weren't a particularly prudish family. When you have an older brother and sister around, and the neighborhood's full of other kids, some of them world-wise beyond their years in their parents' mistaken belief that knowing how to mix a cocktail before you've reached puberty is a proper step toward adulthood, you learn things, you try things.

A little experimenting, I heard my father tell my mother once, after she had found a joint in Wesley's shirt pocket, isn't necessarily a bad thing.

I was thirteen when Wesley lost his mind. He didn't lose it all at once or forever, at least not at the start. He would have "spells." He would have days when he couldn't go to school. That summer, when he was fifteen, it became really apparent to everyone in our world that Wesley was likely broken in a way that he would never "grow out of."

An infamous incident at the Quarry in which Wesley swam naked in front of a couple of dozen of our neighbors pretty much put it up in the sky in big block letters: WESLEY SIMPSON IS CRAZY.

Psychiatrists and a battery of drugs, much more primitive than the ones they have now, failed to do much more than delay the day when Wesley couldn't live with us anymore.

The rest of the family, even my mother, seemed to step away from Wesley, trying to separate themselves from the taint of insanity.

"You know," I heard my mother say once to a friend who was at least feigning sympathy, "I've looked back into my family, and so has Harper, and nobody in either of our families ever had anything like this."

In other words, not our fault. Maybe not Wesley's, but not ours either.

(I have since learned of a great aunt on my father's side who spent her latter years in a "hospital" and a great-grandmother on my mother's side who had to be more or less kept in the cellar.)

Me, I just ached for Wesley. I didn't love him a whit less for his illness, even if it did make him someone different when it was upon him. I tried to make up for what seemed to be a poorly hidden lack of sympathy on the part of Lewis and our parents. Their belief, as crazy as any of Wesley's delusions, was that if someone took him by the shoulders, shook him and ordered him to "pull yourself together," somehow it would all turn out all right.

The summer I turned fourteen, it happened.

We had been fooling around in the basement. I don't know where my parents and Lewis were. When I say "fooling around," I mean everything else but what Wesley called The Final Frontier. Yes, we did oral, too. We convinced ourselves, or Wesley convinced me, that it wasn't really sex, beating Bill Clinton on that one by a few years. We had seen porno flicks that Dad thought were well-hidden. We knew what went where. We knew other kids who were "doing it."

I knew it was wrong, but we just kind of fell into it. I felt guilty, but I felt guilty about refusing Wesley. He needed someone to make him feel good. And, God help me, it made me feel good.

Lewis had a pretty good idea of what was going on, but she was in college by then, so it was just the two of us.

That day, he made me lie on my bed, naked, and then he talked me into letting him tie me up. He'd done it before, and it shamed me to admit how good helplessness felt. The other two times, though, he just felt me up a little, teased me, made me beg.

This time, though, he broke through The Final Frontier.

It didn't hurt that much. There was a little blood, which we cleaned up. He was probably inside me all of two minutes.

But, of course, there are some things you can't take back, some things you can't do just once. . . .

✍

Dec. 12

So finally we come to The Night In Question.

It was still warm that day, somewhere between Labor Day and the beginning of fall, a time I loved, up to that point.

I was sixteen. Wesley was eighteen. He was in one of his several stays at "homes" of one kind or another. This one was just across town. I knew my mother would soon relent and talk my father into letting him come back. They loved Wesley. I'm convinced of that. They just didn't know what to do with him.

When he came back, we always did it. I still had not had sex with another boy. Wesley was all I knew.

Our parents didn't seem to be aware. Lewis would summon me to her room and say things like, "You and Wes must be careful. He's not responsible for his actions, so you've got to be responsible for two." I think she had trouble finding the words for the enormity of what she knew we were doing.

Wesley and I had always kind of teamed up against poor Lewis. I say "poor Lewis" because, even though she was four and six years older than we were, we always seemed to be able to get her goat. Lewis didn't have much of a sense of humor, and I always felt that she didn't think she was as well-liked by our parents as Wesley and I were when we were young, but that's just me.

We would play tricks on her, taking advantage of her when she was supposed to be babysitting us. She would report us to our parents (although she never could bring herself, later, to report on what really needed to be brought to their attention), but they likely as not would tell her that we were just children, to just laugh it off.

That night, our parents were having drinks out on the patio, and I was doing my homework.

Wesley must have slipped away from the group home. I don't think it was too hard. My bedroom had a little side door that opened to the outside, kind of hidden away. I heard a light tapping, and when I looked out, there was Wesley, holding his index finger to his lips.

I let him in. He kissed me and told me that we were going to the Quarry.

I told him that I had homework, but the look of disappointment was enough to make me close my book.

I told my parents I was going up the street to see some friends. They didn't even ask which ones. When they got beyond the second gin and tonic, they didn't ask a lot of probing questions.

I met Wesley out on the street and asked him why we were going to the Quarry. He smiled down at me and said, "So we can be alone."

I didn't resist. I never did, really. We walked downhill until we got to the entrance. I remember that the night was still and sticky, like there was a storm brewing.

We slipped in through the hole in the fence. The water probably was still plenty warm for swimming, but of course Wesley had other ideas.

I was led, willing as a sheep to the slaughter, to the men's dressing room. It still smelled of the damp of summer bathing trunks and the chemicals used when they cleaned the toilet.

I let him strip me and lay me down on the hard wooden bench. He produced some kind of lightweight rope, pulled my hands over my head and tied me to a hook hanging on the wall behind me. When he'd tied me up before, it seemed to be less scary, mostly because we were in our own house.

He teased me a little, with his hands, and something in his eyes, shining from a light pole somewhere in the distance, scared me. He didn't seem like the old Wesley at all anymore.

I begged him to untie me, that I was scared. He said, "You should be," and then he put my panties in my mouth.

And then he had me. He'd had me many times before, of course, but this was different. He was like an animal rutting, grunting and biting as he went at me.

He came twice, and then we heard the patrol car shush-shush-shushing through the gravel.

Wesley motioned for me to be quiet, a superfluous request, since my underwear was in my mouth. He almost appeared to be grinning as he got off me. I thought he was going to untie me, but he just zipped his pants, scooped up my shorts, bra and T-shirt and slipped away, gone into the night.

It seemed like an hour before they found me. I could hear voices the whole time, and was trying to keep quiet, thinking I would prefer to take my chances wriggling free from the ropes sometime before morning, rather than be discovered au naturel *by some of Richmond's finest.*

But it was not to be. The policeman who poked his head in the door didn't seem to see me at first. I suppose he was still a little night-blind. But then he stopped. He said, "Holy shit," and then there were three of them. They seemed as embarrassed as I was as they untied me. Somebody found a robe.

They could see the shape I was in. They could see everything. When they brought the boy in, he looked frightened and confused.

"Is this the one?" one of the cops asked. I could have said he wasn't, but somebody did it, and telling the police the truth seemed too much to bear. In my cowardice, I nodded my head, and they took him away.

I have never since, to this day, seen Richard Slade in person. . . .

Dec. 26

I see, to my amazement, that I am almost finished. I count 152 pages so far. I feel better, even if I don't know what to do with this just yet.

If I give this, my confession, to the police, it will leave a stain on our family name that might never go away.

If I don't, I am doomed. I cannot live any longer with what I have done.

Lewis knows something, and she is afraid, I think. When I mentioned writing "my memoirs," she turned pale and said some things were better left unsaid.

I think she has been snooping around my computer, which is why I have been making printouts as I go along.

The one I feel most sorry for, believe it or not, is Wesley.

How, though, can I be silent any longer?

CHAPTER TWENTY-ONE

I open the front door for Lewis, still not sure where we're going. She doesn't lock it as we leave. I guess this is a pretty safe neighborhood.

She takes her keys out and heads for the Lexus.

"I'll drive," she says.

I ask her where we're going.

"It's not far."

I make sure the recorder in my breast pocket is on and away we go. A couple of turns, and I realize we're on the street above the Quarry. Ahead, I see the home where Lewis, Wesley and Alicia were reared, where I was last seen burglarizing the brick patio and trying to keep Wesley from beating me to death me with a shovel.

Lewis uses the turn signal despite the fact that there probably is no moving vehicle within three blocks of us.

But she doesn't reach the driveway. Instead, she turns just before the fence. There's a long expanse of lawn in front of us, probably a lot that Harper Simpson bought so his nearest neighbors would be a little farther away, or maybe so that one of his kids would build next door someday.

She drives us for maybe fifty yards and then she stops but leaves the engine running. I look back and can see the outline of the big house behind us to my left. We seem to be in some sort of clearing. It's a little warm with the heat on, and I open the passenger side window about halfway. I can feel the winter damp sitting on us like a cold, wet towel.

"Well," Lewis says. "Here we are."

"Where are we?"

"We're at the place where you get to hear the truth, Mr. Black. The jumping-off point, so to speak."

I hear what sounds like a chuckle, but when I look at her face, she isn't smiling. She's staring straight ahead, into the blackness.

"You seem to have it all figured out, Mr. Black," she says. "You're a very clever man. But maybe you don't have it all figured out. Why don't you tell me what you know."

"I can tell you what I suspect."

"That'll do, then."

"I don't think Richard Slade had anything to do with your sister's death."

Lewis turns toward me.

"Well, if not Mr. Slade, then who?"

"I think I know. I think you know. Your brother."

Lewis doesn't deny it, just sighs.

"Let me enlighten you," she says.

"I knew. I pretty much knew right from the start, when they would disappear into one another's bedrooms and not come out for a couple of hours. I should have stopped it, but how do you tell your parents something like that? And they both would have denied it.

"They liked to rub my nose in it, really, the way they would smirk at me, playing grab-ass with each other right in front of me, daring me to confront them with it.

"I never did confront Wesley, but I did try to talk some sense into Alicia. But she would do whatever Wesley wanted her to do. Alicia was easily led."

After what she calls "the incident at the Quarry" and Wesley's disappearance, things were more or less as normal as they apparently ever got around the Simpson household.

"But something would always happen. He'd go off his medication and his illness would start all over again. He told me one time that the drugs made him feel like he was at the bottom of the sea, in the world's heaviest diving suit."

I ask Lewis if she minds if I smoke. I promise I'll blow it out the half-open window.

She starts to say no, then shrugs.

"Why not? What's the harm?"

I suck in the much-needed carcinogens and exhale them into the night like a blue fog.

"You're sure," Lewis asks me, "that you can't be persuaded to part with Alicia's manuscript? I've read it already, you know."

Alicia had suspected that, so I'm not all that surprised.

I tell her that, for the time being, I'd prefer to keep it.

"As you wish."

She cracks her window an inch or two. Even with mine half-open, it's getting pretty warm in here.

"Well," she says, "then I guess you might as well know everything. Confession is good for the soul."

She surprises me by taking the Camel from my mouth, taking a big drag.

"I quit ten years ago," she says, "but you never lose the itch, do you?"

I concede that you apparently don't.

She hands the cigarette back.

"I thought the whole mess was over. It had receded into the past until it had almost vanished from sight."

She told me that Alicia hadn't seemed to be fazed much when the story first broke. But when it became more and more obvious that Richard Slade had not raped her, that he had been in prison all those years because of a case of mistaken identity, she became more and more withdrawn.

"Then, last Thanksgiving, she told me she was writing her 'memoirs.' I tried to talk her out of it, but she wouldn't listen. She said confession was good for the soul, and I told her that was a crock, that confession was good for nothing but ruining a perfectly good life."

Lewis sighs, looking straight ahead. I don't think she's even talking to me now. She might not even know I'm here.

"She just stared at me. And then you know what she said? She said, 'You think this has been a perfectly good life? You think hell is a perfectly good life?'

"I had always thought there was more to the story than Alicia let on, even back when it first happened, but I was still fool enough to think it was just her feeling guilty about maybe being mistaken, maybe sending the wrong man to prison for the rest of his life.

"I thought that right up to the time I finally got to read what she had written. How could I have been so stupid?"

All through the holidays, Alicia was writing. She didn't try very hard to hide the fact, Lewis said. When asked about what exactly she was writing, Alicia just smiled and said, "The truth."

"I tried to stop her," Lewis says, "and she told me at one point that she had quit. But I knew she hadn't."

The wind is starting to pick up. I pitch the butt out the window and roll it up a little.

The day after Richard Slade was officially exonerated by the state, Alicia went to the gym. She left to work out at five every morning. That, a little grocery shopping and meetings of various charity boards she was on comprised most of her time away from the home where she had spent most of her life. If she lived in a bigger town with meaner or at least less lazy media types, her front lawn would have been strewn with cameramen and talking heads all night.

Lewis says she used her key to get into her parents' old house. She went up to Alicia's study and got on her computer. Alicia apparently hadn't tried to hide anything.

"She hadn't changed her password in the last ten years, when she told me what it was—Simpson. All I had to do was log in, and there, on her desktop, was a folder that said, 'Confession.'

"I took a glance at the first chapter, and I knew what it was."

There were some disks in the drawer, so Lewis made a copy and left.

"That night, after Carl went to bed, I went to my laptop and started reading. By the time I was finished, light was coming in the window, and I knew everything. Everything I never wanted anyone else to know."

The next day, a Wednesday, she went to her parents' home again before dawn, went back to the computer and erased everything.

She sighs.

"Except, of course, that my careless little sister wasn't so careless after all. She had copied everything. Hell, she probably even has it copied on a disk somewhere, although I haven't been able to find it. When I told her I had erased everything, that it was for her own good, she just smiled and shrugged her shoulders. She said she'd just go to the police and the newspaper and tell them everything. She was beyond caring, Mr. Black.

"I knew what I had to do."

I hesitate to break the spell. It's always good to let the subject talk for as long as he or she wants, give them enough rope for a proper hanging. Sometimes, I feel like a shrink or a priest. But I have to ask.

"So, when did you tell Wesley about all this?"

She looks at me like I'm speaking Urdu. She laughs.

"Wesley didn't know anything about all this until yesterday," she says.

"But he knew all along the wrong man was in prison."

"I don't know what Wesley knew. He seemed so sane at times, but then he'd go into some tirade about 'those black bastards' who raped Alicia, and I really wondered if he knew at all, or if it was just somebody else inhabiting his body that night. Somebody else inhabited his body a lot, especially back then, before the drugs got better."

It wasn't that hard, the way Lewis explains it. Carl kept a variety of guns around the house, collected over the years. Lewis had gone out with him to the firing range on occasion. He had one gun, a Colt, that he used to brag he'd gotten from a guy his firm represented. It was completely untraceable. Carl joked that this was the one he'd use if he ever had to kill somebody.

"He's still not aware it's missing," she says. Her laugh is as dry as an Arab's umbrella.

"I just sat there, at that light at Cary and Meadow. Thursday morning, the light was green when she went through. Friday morning, the same thing.

"Then, on Saturday, I looked in the rearview mirror and saw her Acura coming down the street. About half a block before she got there, just when I thought I'd wasted another night's sleep, the light turned to yellow. Alicia might have run it, but she didn't."

Lewis was parked on the left side of the street, just before the light. When Alicia stopped, Lewis got out of her car, ran the twenty feet between her and her sister and tapped on Alicia's window.

"She seemed surprised, and then she recognized me, and she rolled down the window.

"And then I shot her. Three times. I don't think she really felt anything. At least, I hope not."

How humane, I'm thinking.

"You see," Lewis says, turning to face me, talking to me again, "I couldn't let her do it. I couldn't let her ruin us like that."

I'm thinking that things are pretty much in the crapper for the Simpson-Witts anyhow. She seems to have read my mind.

"I tried," she says. "But there's just too much out there now. It would be like trying to put water back in a vase after it's spilled. There's nothing left to do now. Except this."

I'm getting a little uneasy about what "this" might be.

"Um, maybe we could make some kind of arrangements. About the manuscript."

She doesn't even bother to laugh this time.

"No, Mr. Black. This is it. You'll never give Alicia's manuscript back. And Carl will, someday soon, realize that his prized Colt is gone. He might cover for me, but I've considered the odds, and the chances of that damn confession not seeing the light of day, compounded by the chances of Carl not reporting that gun missing and solving the big mystery of who shot Alicia, are not very good at all.

"I hope my children will forgive me. But now I'm very tired, Mr. Black."

I ask her if she wants me to drive back.

"I don't think so," she says, as I slowly, quiet as a mouse, reach for the door handle. I've already released the seat belt. My eyes have adjusted to the darkness, and I can see that what lies directly ahead of us is space. The yard seems to slope downward a few feet in front of us and then disappear into nothingness. I am fully aware, for the first time, of what lies beyond and beneath us.

"Mr. Black," Lewis Witt says, "did you ever see that movie, *Thelma and Louise?*"

I've already rolled the window back down. But when I push on the door handle, I learn to my great regret that Lewis has put the childproof lock on. I give up all pretense and subtlety. My pleas and promises bounce off her.

"Here we go," Lewis says. She slips the car into drive.

As the car starts moving forward, slowly at first, I have only one option.

I once rode in a pace car at the NASCAR track in town. They were giving all the reporters free rides, probably because they liked to torture helpless creatures. There are no doors on those damn things. You have to climb in through the window and then climb back out again. I still have the hoary image of a fat woman sportswriter wedged halfway in, halfway out, her butt blotting out the sun, imbedded in my brain. When I'm trying to be good, I think of her.

So, for the second time in my life, I attempt to leave a car via the passenger-side window. It seems to take forever, and I can feel the car gain momentum. When I finally throw myself, head first, to freedom, I'm tumbling downhill. It doesn't feel like good luck, but a tulip poplar stops me ten feet from the edge. I scream like a little girl when my already abused ribs collide with the tree's thickness, but it saves me.

I hear the roar of an engine and then a second of silence as Lewis Witt leaves solid ground.

The sound, when the Lexus hits the water fifty feet below, is as cold and final as a death rattle.

CHAPTER TWENTY-TWO

Thursday, February 10th

McGrumpy, the Prestwould's self-appointed wit, refers to our unit as General Hospital.

Good thing McGrumpy isn't funnier. It hurts like a bitch to laugh.

Andi's doing better and should be able to face the world unaided by her feckless father in a few days.

Me, I look like King Tut. All this crap wrapped around me keeps my ribs intact, I guess. Now, if I could only breathe. And scratch that spot on my back.

Custalow's a prince. I think he's giving preferential treatment to my daughter, but he's doing a pretty good job of playing nursemaid to me, too. It wouldn't surprise me if Abe wasn't looking for another place to live, somewhere that you don't have to take care of a pair of semi-impaired adults.

All in all, though, I don't have much to complain about. I am, after all, aboveground.

As Peggy used to say (often, I thought, without much evidence to back it up), things could be worse.

It has been six days since Lewis Witt's Lexus did an Olympic swan dive into the Quarry. It felt like I was going close to the legal speed limit when I hit that tulip poplar like a crash-test dummy.

I remember hearing the car hitting the water, and then I must have blacked out. The next thing I know, there are sirens blaring and flashing lights everywhere. I managed to crawl a few feet until I could see over the lip to the cluster-fuck below.

Somebody down there must have called 911 when they heard the Lexus hit, and by the time I looked, half the city's paid employees seemed to be in attendance. The lights were playing on the Quarry's water, turning it all red and blue like a Fourth of July fireworks show. I could make out the rear end of the last car Lewis Witt would ever drive, its license plate poking out. It landed in a shallow spot near the edge.

I reached Custalow on my cellphone, which took a mauling and kept on calling. I think I told him to get me the hell out of there. But before Abe could ride to my rescue, the cops found me.

It didn't take Richmond's finest too long to figure out that the aquatic Lexus didn't fall from outer space. Eventually, they found their way to the side yard of the late Harper and Simone Simpson.

I was lying there, wondering why there were two moons out tonight, when the sky was blocked out by an impressive beer belly.

"I might have known your ass would be involved in this somehow," a familiar voice said.

Gillespie.

I tried to say something smart, but talking, as well as breathing, was becoming kind of hard. I felt like somebody had beaten me with a tire iron. Inexplicably, in the middle of all the hubbub, Sarah Goodnight appeared and rode with me to the hospital.

They stationed a cop outside my room and gave me plenty of what would have been, under better circumstances, outstanding party drugs. I slept between nightmares.

Two police officers came around the next day. They haven't been too happy with me since the unfortunate incident with the late, unlamented David Junior Shiflett. I had the feeling they were dying to make me more complicit than I was in the death of Lewis Witt.

Fortunately for me, another item in my jacket pocket also proved to be too tough to kill. The recorder caught enough of what Lewis said to convince the cops that they didn't have a prayer of convicting me for anything worth the trouble.

Even the chief himself came by. I've known L. D. Jones since high school, and he doesn't really wish me any permanent harm.

He wanted to know if I still had the manuscript. I told him that I had burned it. He told me he didn't believe that. I told him to prove it.

"Well," the chief said, "this is a mess. And now we've got the brother to deal with."

Sometime after dawn the next day, one of the cops on the scene at the Quarry, perhaps trying to figure out how to get that Lexus out of the city's most exclusive swimming hole, decided to use the facilities.

When he opened the door to the men's dressing room, there hung Wesley Simpson.

They figured later that he'd been there about two days. He'd tied one end of a rope to a hook overhead, stood up on one of the worn-out benches and tied the other end around his neck. From the scuff marks on the floor below, he almost left himself too much rope to be successful. Almost. I guess close doesn't count in horseshoes and hangings.

They couldn't find a suicide note. My guess, which I kept to myself, was that Lewis told him the jig was up, and he couldn't take it. Being held up as a guy who had committed incest with, or even raped, his baby sister, and then let some black kid take the rap and go to prison for half his life for the crime was, I'm guessing, more than the shaky equilibrium of Wesley Simpson could handle.

Or maybe he just missed Alicia. The photo of the two of them lay at his feet, undisturbed since I'd first seen it.

I'm certain that Lewis knew her brother was dead when she took me for that little joy ride. Maybe she thought it was time to end everything. Maybe she could see that there was no way out of what might have been worse for her than death—shame and dishonor.

I doubt if Carl and her kids would agree with her right now.

There wasn't any reason to keep Richard Slade in jail, but still they waited five days to release him. It took the cops and prosecutor that long to go through all the stages of grief at having arrested the wrong man twice. They finally arrived at "acceptance" yesterday morning.

By then, I was able to join Kate and Marcus Green for Richard's second coming-out party.

Slade was the same decent, honest man he'd been for twenty-eight years in the penal system and during his sojourn as a suspected murderer. He thanked God. He thanked the police. He thanked his mother, as Philomena stood beside him and wiped the only tear I've ever seen her shed, with the TV cameras recording it all. He thanked Kate and Marcus. He even thanked me. Journalist gets thanked. Stop the presses.

And then he and his mother got into Chanelle's car and headed east, toward home.

Kate was standing beside me when they disappeared around the corner.

"Well," she said, "I guess you've got your story."

I told her that, yeah, I had my story. Well, mine and Sarah Goodnight's. Because she was on night cops, she had been on duty when word came in about an "incident" at the Quarry. She knew where I was going that night, and she had her suspicions that I was somehow in the middle of it all. She drove out there and got what information she could for the Saturday paper. Unnamed victim's car does a face-first into the water. No motive. No body recovered yet.

But Sarah heard another siren and realized that it was going not to the Quarry but to the hill above it. She got into her car and followed the flashing lights.

I was still there, being packed into the back of the ambulance. When she saw it was me, she ran over. I was afraid she was going to hug my poor, aching ribs, something I definitely didn't want right then.

Somehow, she got them to let her ride to the hospital with me. I told her everything she needed to know, including the name of the driver of the car now at the bottom of the Quarry, which she had already guessed.

As soon as we reached the hospital, she scurried off and got Baer out of bed to give her a ride to the paper, where she wrote the story nobody else had. Or at least as much of it as she knew. I like Sarah, but not enough to tell her everything.

She did follow-ups the next four days. She got to tell our breathless readers about Wesley Simpson's suicide, although she had to give that one to the freeloaders via our website.

Yesterday, though, I told her I was taking over. She didn't argue.

So, I was out there on a February morning as clean and crisp as a good Sauvignon Blanc, with a slight bouquet of impending spring, watching Richard Slade ride off to freedom again.

Even Marcus Green thanked me.

"For what?" I asked him. "Now you don't have a chance to undress some dumb-ass prosecutor in a courtroom. You've missed one of the biggest roles of your acting career."

"Some things," he said, "are more important than a big day in court."

I almost think he meant it.

Kate and I had coffee and bagels afterward at Perly's. Outside the front door, a panhandler put his hand on my arm. His dark skin seemed to have faded to gray in the stingy winter light. He might have been thirty or sixty. I started to brush him away when he stepped back and said, "Thanks, man. For Richard Slade."

It made the broken ribs hurt a little less.

I gave him a buck.

Inside, I posted the story between sips.

Finally, I shut the laptop and looked over at Kate.

"Nice job," she said.

She brought me up to speed on where I am in the quest to get my driver's license back. It seems the city takes a dim view of people ignoring its one-way signs and abusing its alcohol. This is going to be expensive, Kate assured me. I might be able to drive only on work-related trips, and I would be expected to submit to some bad-driver classes, for which I also would pay dearly. And they probably would expect me to join AA.

I said nothing about that last one. As always, I can quit any time I want. I've barely had a drink since Saturday.

She told me not to worry about her costs.

"Pro bono is my middle name," is the way she put it.

I reached across and put my hand on top of hers, managing to smear my sleeve with cream cheese. She surprised me by drawing her hand back and putting it in her lap. And I thought things were going so well.

"Willie," she said, and then paused.

Please, please, please don't say we have to talk, I thought to myself.

"We have to talk."

And then she told me how she and Greg had indeed reconciled. All was well at Chez Ellis.

"What we did . . ." she began, leaving it there for me to finish.

Don't worry, I told her, it'll be our little secret. Ships passing in the night and all that crap.

"No," she said, "it was more than that. I'm still attracted to you, Willie. But I do love Greg. We want to have a family. You know."

Yeah, I know. I take a long sip, silently count to three, and make my pitch for the sportsmanship award. This year's Best Loser trophy goes to Willie Black, who assured his ex-wife that he is happy for her happiness, caring nothing for his own.

And so we parted, promising to stay in touch. I told her I would walk down to the paper and write something for tomorrow's edition. When she said goodbye, I waved without looking back and fumbled for a Camel.

They were expecting me in the newsroom. It was hard not to attract attention, in my mummy garb. I had to stop three women and a couple of guys from hugging my aching ribs. Sally Velez promised to buy me a drink. I told her I'd take a rain check. Enos Jackson looked up from his desk and gave me a thumbs-up. Mal Wheelwright came out of his office to shake my hand and welcome me back.

So maybe, I thought to myself, I am back. Baer came up, almost teary-eyed, and thanked me for saving his job. I'm sure he'd be even more grateful if it had been him instead of Sarah who got to tell our faithful readers about it.

Don't think a thing about it, I told him. Really. Nothing I wouldn't have done for any asshole.

"I need to see you for a minute," Wheelie said as I was exchanging pleasantries with various other staffers.

Almost got away clean.

When I walked into the managing editor's office, he told me that Grubby wanted to talk to me.

"He said to bring you up there ASAP."

On the suit floor, Sandy McCool told me she was glad to see me back and in one piece, and that Mr. Grubbs would see us momentarily. Sandy, as usual, gave nothing away.

When we were finally summoned, it wasn't to Grubby's office but to a conference room two doors down.

"Oh, man," Wheelie said when we were directed to the room. "This is where the nut-cutting happens."

Wheelie obviously had been here before.

He opened the door carefully, as if he thought a tiger might leap out.

Inside the room were James H. Grubbs and his ultimate boss, Giles Whitehurst. Neither of them stood when we entered.

Grubby motioned for us to sit across from him at a table that could have seated twelve. Giles Whitehurst sat at the end, a good ten feet from the rest of us.

"Willie," Grubby said, "you know Mr. Whitehurst."

I nodded. It hadn't been six days since he told me, from the comfort of his Windsor Farms den, what the consequences would be if I persisted in harassing Lewis Witt and her family. And now she was dead, no doubt driven to her demise by my snooping.

"Mr. Black," Whitehurst said, "you don't follow directions very well, do you?"

Well, there was nothing to lose by this point. What was he going to do besides fire me? Shoot me with two people watching? Besides, my ribs were hurting and my ass was starting to itch thinking about what this fucker was trying to cover up.

"Not when they involve obstructing justice."

Wheelie gave me a little sideways kick under the table. I kicked him back, which made my ribs ache more. Grubby just shook his head slightly.

Whitehurst laughed, but nobody else did.

"So you think I've been obstructing justice?"

"You did everything you could to keep an innocent man in prison. Yeah, I think that pretty much sums it up. Obstruction of fucking justice."

Whitehurst obviously wasn't used to being talked to like this. Me, I just wanted to get it over with. Fire me so I can really tell you what I think of you.

I thought he might just do the deed right there, all neat and clean. But guys like Giles Whitehurst don't have to do it face-to-face. They can always pay somebody else to stick in the shiv.

"Well," he said, "I just wanted to see you one more time. We've been talking about you. James here will fill you in."

And then he left, closing the door behind him so softly we barely heard it.

I turned to Grubby.

"James?"

"Shut up. You're lucky you still have a job."

"I still have a job?"

"For now. You can thank Mr. Whitehurst for that."

I didn't really feel inclined to thanks Giles Whitehurst for much of anything, but paychecks are nice to have. Maybe I'll send him a card.

As it turns out, our board chairman apparently had more loyalty to his own reputation than he did to the family of Alicia Simpson and Lewis Witt. When he found out exactly what happened twenty-eight years ago at the Philadelphia Quarry and what happened January 22nd at a stoplight on West Cary, I guess he just didn't care to soil his well-manicured hands with it anymore.

He probably thought that the first thing I'd do, after he fired my ass, would be to take it to our local free weekly, maybe blog about it. Hell, he probably thought I'd peddle it to the *Washington Post.*

He might have been right.

Grubby told me to start writing "if you can stay sober and healthy long enough to do it. Maybe Baer can help you."

I told Grubby what he could do with Baer's help. He told me to watch it. I got up to leave.

"Oh, one more thing," he said as Wheelie held the door open for me, anxious for both of us to get the hell out of there. "What did you do with the manuscript?"

I told him the same thing I told the cops.

The story was in this morning's paper. I'll do something more long-winded on Sunday, the infamous, tree-killing tick-tock, but most of it was laid out for our paying customers today. We didn't post this one on the website until it landed on people's doorsteps, a rare victory for print, whose won-lost record lately is in Wile E. Coyote territory. Grubby thought it would increase rack sales to not give this one away online. W touted it in yesterday's paper ("What really happened to Alicia Simpson?") and printed a few thousand extra.

Most of the story was there. The arrest and conviction of Richard Slade in 1983. The DNA evidence that proved he didn't do it. Alicia Simpson's murder and Slade's second arrest. Lewis Witt's half-gainer into the Quarry. Her brother's suicide. Slade's release.

I have to admit, the lede wasn't half-bad:

"On a cold, stark February night, on a bluff overlooking the place where everything began and where her brother's lifeless body hung still undiscovered, Lewis Simpson Witt explained why she murdered her sister."

If that doesn't sell some papers, I'll kiss your ass.

Sally Velez thought I should delete "lifeless" and "still" and not start with consecutive prepositional phrases. I told her she didn't have an ounce of poetry in her editor's soul. She told me most of our readers aren't really into poetry, but she let it stand.

I didn't go that deep into the details of the manuscript. There was enough, though, for the average reader to understand what happened and why. I didn't see any point in quoting long stretches verbatim from Alicia Simpson's revelation of the shame that had cast a shadow on her life and stolen much of Richard Slade's. Grubby and Wheelie were both a little put out that I had destroyed the manuscript. But we have Lewis Witt's final confession on tape. That's enough.

Lewis Witt's husband and children have suffered enough. I can imagine the kids all moving away, somewhere where nobody's ever heard of Alicia Simpson or Richard Slade. I can imagine Carl staying because he's too old to start over, still going to the club and having drinks with friends, but in a world much diminished, with the whispers swarming around him like gnats he can never swat away.

In a perfect world, I would spare them that grief. In a perfect world, though, a man like Richard Slade would not spend twenty-eight years in prison for something he didn't do and then face the prospect of going back again. In a perfect world, imperfect men like me wouldn't have to be in a position to help the world pass judgment.

I am not a cruel man, but I am a purebred, flea-bitten news-hound. Sometimes, I wish Whoever amuses Himself by watching us fetch the truth would throw that stick for someone else to chase. Me, I can never resist going after it and then returning for a pat on the head.

About that manuscript. I'm a pack rat. I still have my 1958 Topps baseball card collection. Do you think I'd burn Alicia Simpson's confession?

Today is family reunion day, sort of.

Philomena Slade called me late yesterday afternoon at the paper, while I was writing the story. She invited me to come for her son's second coming-home celebration in less than four weeks.

I asked her if I could bring Peggy. When my drug-addled mother came by to see me on Tuesday, she again expressed a desire to see Momma Phil, whom she hasn't laid eyes on in decades. I suppose there's some sense of reconnecting. Maybe she thinks the long-departed Artie Lee's first cousin can tell her something she doesn't already know about my late father. Maybe she just wants to go for a ride.

At any rate, Philomena said that would be grand. Something about the way she said "grand" just killed me.

So here we sit, in a living room that's about four people over what the fire department would recommend. Peggy and Les are here, with the latter looking a little out of place but otherwise happy as if he had good sense. Chanelle has brought Jamal and Jeroy, who are both sitting on their uncle Richard's lap, giggling as they try to get away. Half the neighborhood drops by, in twos and threes, and there never seem to be fewer than twenty people in that small room. Bump Freeman even stops in, shy and uncertain at the door, and is greeted as warmly as a brother.

Abe drove, with Andi in the front seat, and Peggy, Les and me in the back. Abe's sitting on a chair that's about three sizes too small and might collapse if he eats one more drumstick, talking with Richard about the good ol' days in stir, I suppose.

Andi has never met this side of the family before. She's in a long conversation with Chanelle. I think they're talking about hair. Philomena and Peggy act as if they're just picking up on a conversation they abandoned a few minutes ago instead of nearly half a century back. Momma Phil has a photo album out, and Peggy, barely stoned, is staring at it intently, reaching up once or twice to wipe her eyes.

My ribs are aching a little. Andi's probably going to have to punt this semester, moving her theoretical graduation farther into the future. The paper's announced that it's going to "give" the staff two "furlough" days a month, for which we won't get paid but probably will still wind up working, because somebody's got to do it.

But in a brief lull, my daughter reaches over, takes my hand and squeezes it, and I know Peggy's right.

Things could be worse.